William Makepeace Thackeray

The Rose and the Ring; or, the History of Prince Giglio and Prince Bulbo

A Fire-Side Pantomime for Great and Small Children

William Makepeace Thackeray

The Rose and the Ring; or, the History of Prince Giglio and Prince Bulbo
A Fire-Side Pantomime for Great and Small Children

ISBN/EAN: 9783337165376

Printed in Europe, USA, Canada, Australia, Japan

Cover: Foto ©Andreas Hilbeck / pixelio.de

More available books at **www.hansebooks.com**

POOR BULBO IS ORDERED FOR EXECUTION

OR, THE

HISTORY OF PRINCE GIGLIO AND PRINCE BULBO.

A Fireside Pantomime for Great and Small Children.

By W. M. THACKERAY,

AUTHOR OF "VANITY FAIR," "HENRY ESMOND," "ENGLISH HUMORISTS,"
"THE GREAT HOGGARTY DIAMOND," ETC.

BOSTON
ESTES AND LAURIAT,
301-305 WASHINGTON STREET.
1883.

PRELUDE.

It happened that the undersigned spent the last Christmas season in a foreign city, where there were many English children.

In that city, if you wanted to give a child's party, you could not even get a magic lantern or buy Twelfth-Night characters—those funny painted pictures of the King, the Queen, the Lover, the Lady, the Dandy, the Captain, and so on—with which our young ones are wont to recreate themselves at this festive time.

My friend Miss Bunch, who was governess of a large family that lived in the *Piano Nobile* of the house inhabited by myself and my young charges (it was the Palazzo Poniatowski at Rome, and Messrs. Spillmann, two of the best pastry-cooks in Christendom, have their shop on the ground floor)—Miss Bunch, I say, begged me to draw a set of Twelfth-Night characters for the amusement of our young people.

She is a lady of great fancy and droll imagination, and having looked at the characters, she and I composed a history about them, which was recited to the little folks at night, and served as our FIRESIDE PANTOMIME.

Our juvenile audience was amused by the adventures of Giglio and Bulbo, Rosalba and Angelica. I am bound to say, the fate

of the Hall Porter created a considerable sensation ; and the wrath
of Countess Gruffanuff was received with extreme pleasure.

If these children are pleased, thought I, why should not others
be amused also?   In a few days, Dr. Birch's young friends will be
expected to reassemble at Rodwell Regis, where they will learn
every thing that is useful, and, under the eyes of careful ushers,
continue the business of their little lives.

But in the mean while, and for a brief holiday, let us laugh and
be as pleasant as we can.   And you elder folks—a little joking,
and dancing, and fooling, will do even you no harm.   The author
wishes you a merry Christmas, and welcomes you to the Fireside
Pantomime.

M. A. TITMARSH.

DECEMBER, 1854.

THE ROSE AND THE RING.

I.

SHOWS HOW THE ROYAL FAMILY SAT DOWN TO BREAKFAST.

THIS is Valoroso XXIV., King of Paflagonia, seated with his queen and only child at their royal breakfast-table, and receiving the letter which announces to his majesty a proposed visit from Prince Bulbo, heir of Padella, reigning king of Crim Tartary. Remark the delight upon the monarch's royal features. He is so absorbed in the perusal of the King of Crim Tartary's letter, that he allows his eggs to get cold, and leaves his august muffins untasted.

"What! that wicked, brave, delightful Prince Bulbo!" cries Princess Angelica: "so handsome, so accomplished, so witty—the conqueror of Rimbombamento, where he slew ten thousand giants!"

"Who told you of him, my dear?" asks his majesty.

"A little bird," says Angelica.

"Poor Giglio!" says mamma, pouring out the tea.

"Bother Giglio!" cries Angelica, tossing up her head, which rustled with a thousand curl-papers.

"I wish," growls the king, "I wish Giglio was . . . . ."

"Was better? Yes, dear, he is better," says the queen. "Angelica's little maid, Betsinda, told me so when she came to my room this morning with my early tea."

"You are always drinking tea," said the monarch, with a scowl.

"It is better than drinking port, or brandy and water," replies her majesty.

"Well, well, my dear, I only said you were fond of drinking tea," said the King of Paflagonia, with an effort as if to command his temper. "Angelica! I hope you have plenty of new dresses; your milliners' bills are long enough. My dear queen, you must see and have some parties. I prefer dinners, but of course you will be for balls. Your everlasting blue velvet quite tires me; and, my love, I should like you to have a new necklace. Order one. Not more than a hundred or a hundred and fifty thousand pounds."

"And Giglio, dear?" says the queen.

"GIGLIO MAY GO TO THE—"

"Oh, sir," screams her majesty. "Your own nephew! our late king's only son!"

"Giglio may go to the tailor's, and order the bills to be sent in to Glumboso to pay. Confound him! I mean, bless his dear heart. He need want for nothing; give him a couple of guineas for pocket money, my dear; and you may as well order yourself bracelets, while you are about the necklace, Mrs. V."

Her Majesty, or *Mrs. V.*, as the monarch facetiously called her (for even royalty will have its sport, and this august family were very much attached), embraced her husband, and, twining her arm round her daughter's waist, they quitted the breakfast-room in order to make all things ready for the princely stranger.

When they were gone, the smile that had lighted up the eyes of the *husband* and *father* fled—the pride of the *King* fled—the MAN was alone. Had I the pen of a G. P. R. James, I would also depict his flashing eye, his distended nostril—his dressing-gown, pocket-hand-kerchief, and boots. But I need not say I have *not* the pen of that novelist; suffice it to say, Valoroso was alone.

He rushed to the cupboard, seizing from the table one of the many egg-cups with which his princely board was served for the matin meal, drew out a bottle of right Nantz or Cognac, filled and emptied the cup several times, and laid it down with a hoarse " Ha, ha, ha! now Valoroso is a man again!"

" But oh!" he went on (still sipping, I am sorry to say), " ere I was a king, I needed not this intoxicating draught; once I detested the hot brandy wine, and quaffed no other fount but nature's rill. It dashes not more quickly o'er the rocks, than I did, as, with blunderbuss in hand, I brushed away the early morning dew, and shot the partridge, snipe, or antlered deer! Ah! well may England's dramatist remark, 'Uneasy lies the head that wears a crown!' Why did I steal my nephew's, my young Giglio's— Steal! said I ; no, no, no, not steal, not steal. Let me withdraw that odious expression. I took, and on my manly head I set, the royal crown of Paflagonia ; I took, and with my royal arm I wield, the sceptral rod of Paflagonia ; I took, and in my outstretched hand I hold, the royal orb of Paflagonia! Could a poor boy, a sniveling, driveling boy—was in his nurse's arms but yes-terday, and cried for sugar-plums and puled for pap—bear up the aw-ful weight of crown, orb, sceptre ? gird on the sword my royal fathers wore, and meet in fight the tough Crimean foe ?"

And then the monarch went on to argue in his own mind (though we need not say that blank verse is not argument) that what he had got it was his duty to keep, and that, if at one time he had entertained ideas of a certain restitution, which shall be nameless, the prospect by a *certain marriage* of uniting two crowns and two nations which had been engaged in bloody and expensive wars, as the Paflagonians and Crimeans had been, put the idea of Giglio's restoration to the throne out of the question : nay, were his own brother, King Savio alive, he would certainly will away the crown from his own son in order to bring about such a desirable union.

Thus easily do we deceive ourselves! Thus do we fancy what we wish is right! The king took courage, read the papers, finished his muffins and eggs, and rang the bell for his prime minister. The queen, after thinking whether she should go up and see Giglio, who had been sick, thought, " Not now. Business first; pleasure afterward. I will go and see dear Giglio this afternoon ; and now I will drive to the jeweler's, to look for the necklace and bracelets." The princess went up into her own room, and made Betsinda, her maid, bring out all her dresses ; and as for Giglio, they forgot him as much as I forget what I had for dinner last Tuesday twelvemonth.

II.

HOW KING VALOROSO GOT THE CROWN, AND PRINCE GIGLIO WENT WITHOUT.

PAFLAGONIA, ten or twenty thousand years ago, appears to have been one of those kingdoms where the laws of succession were not settled; for when King Savio died, leaving his brother regent of the kingdom, and guardian of Savio's orphan infant, this unfaithful regent took no sort of regard of the late monarch's will; had himself proclaimed sovereign of Paflagonia under the title of King Valoroso XXIV., had a most splendid coronation, and ordered all the nobles of the kingdom to pay him homage. So long as Valoroso gave them plenty of balls at court, plenty of money, and lucrative places, the Paflagonian nobility did not care who was king; and as for the people in those early times, they were equally indifferent. The Prince Giglio, by reason of his tender age at his royal father's death, did not feel the loss of his crown and empire. As long as he had plenty of toys and sweetmeats, a holiday five times a week, and a horse and gun to go out shooting when he grew a little older, and, above all, the company of his darling cousin, the king's only child, poor Giglio was perfectly contented; nor did he envy his uncle the royal robes and sceptre, the great, hot, uncomfortable throne of state, and the enormous, cumbersome crown in which that monarch appeared from morning till night. King Valoroso's portrait has been left to us, and I think you will agree with me that he must have been sometimes *rather tired* of his velvet.

and his diamonds, and his ermine, and his grandeur. I shouldn't like
to sit in that stifling robe with such a thing as that on my head.

No doubt, the queen must have been lovely in her youth; for
though she grew rather stout in after life, yet her features, as shown

in her portrait, are certainly *pleasing*. If she was fond of flattery, scandal, cards, and fine clothes, let us deal gently with her infirmities, which, after all, may be no greater than our own. She was kind to her nephew ; and if she had any scruples of conscience about her husband's taking the young prince's crown, consoled herself by thinking that the king, though a usurper, was a most respectable man, and that at his death Prince Giglio would be restored to his throne, and share it with his cousin, whom he loved so fondly.

The prime minister was Glumboso, an old statesman, who most cheerfully swore fidelity to King Valoroso, and in whose hands the monarch left all the affairs of his kingdom. All Valoroso wanted was plenty of money, plenty of hunting, plenty of flattery, and as little trouble as possible. As long as he had his sport, this monarch cared little how his people paid for it. He engaged in some wars, and, of course, the Paflagonian newspapers announced that he gained prodigious victories ; he had statues erected to himself in every city of the empire ; and, of course, his pictures placed every where, and in all the print-shops : he was Valoroso the Magnanimous, Valoroso the Victorious, Valoroso the Great, and so forth ; for even in these early times courtiers and people knew how to flatter.

This royal pair had one only child, the Princess Angelica, who, you may be sure, was a paragon in the courtiers' eyes, in her parents', and in her own. It was said she had the longest hair, the largest eyes, the slimmest waist, the smallest foot, and the most lovely complexion of any young lady in the Paflagonian dominions. Her accomplishments were announced to be even superior to her beauty ; and governesses used to shame their idle pupils by telling them what Princess Angelica could do. She could play the most difficult pieces of music at sight. She could answer any one of Mangnal's Questions. She knew every date in the history of Paflagonia and every other country. She knew French, English, Italian, German, Spanish, Hebrew, Greek, Latin, Cappadocian, Samothracian, Ægean, and Crim Tartar. In a word, she was a most accomplished young creature ; and her governess and lady-in-waiting was the severe Countess Gruffanuff.

Would you not fancy, from this picture, that Gruffanuff must have been a person of the highest birth ? She looks so haughty, that I should have thought her a princess at the very least, with a pedigree

reaching as far back as the deluge.   But this lady was no better born
than many other ladies who give themselves airs, and all sensible
people laughed at her absurd pretensions ; the fact is, she had been
maid-servant to the queen when her majesty was only princess, and
her husband had been head footman, but after his death or *disappear-*
ance, of which you shall hear presently, this Mrs. Gruffanuff, by flattering, toadying, and wheedling her royal mistress, became a favorite
with the queen (who was rather a weak woman) ; and her majesty
gave her a title, and made her nursery governess to the princess.

And now I must tell you about the princess's learning and accomplishments, for which she had such a wonderful character.   Clever
Angelica certainly was, but as *idle as possible*.   Play at sight, indeed !
she could play one or two pieces, and pretend that she had never seen
them before ; she could answer half a dozen Mangnal's Questions ;
but then you must take care to ask the *right* ones.   As for her languages, she had masters in plenty, but I doubt whether she knew
more than a few phrases in each, for all her pretense ; and as for her
embroidery and her drawing, she showed beautiful specimens, it is
true, but *who did them ?*

This obliges me to tell the truth, and to do so I must go back ever
so far, and tell you about the FAIRY BLACKSTICK.

III.

TELLS WHO THE FAIRY BLACKSTICK WAS, AND WHO WERE EVER SO MANY GRAND PERSONAGES BESIDES.

BETWEEN the kingdoms of Paflagonia and Crim Tartary there lived a mysterious personage, who was known in those countries as the Fairy Blackstick, from the ebony wand or crutch which she carried; on which she rode to the moon sometimes, or upon other excursions of business or pleasure, and with which she performed her wonders.

When she was young, and had been first taught the art of conjuring by the necromancer, her father, she was always practicing her skill, whizzing about from one kingdom to another upon her black stick, and conferring her fairy favors upon this prince or that. She had scores of royal godchildren; turned numberless wicked people into beasts, birds, millstones, clocks, pumps, bootjacks, umbrellas, or other absurd shapes; and, in a word, was one of the most active and oflicious of the whole college of fairies.

But after two or three thousand years of this sport. I suppose Blackstick grew tired of it. , Or perhaps she thought, "What good am I doing by sending this princess to sleep for a hundred years? by fixing a black pudding on to that booby's nose? by causing diamonds and pearls to drop from one little girl's mouth, and vipers and toads from another's? I begin to think I do as much harm as good by my perform-

B

ances. I might as well shut my incantations up, and allow things to
take their natural course.

"There were my two young goddaughters, King Savio's wife and
Duke Padella's wife, I gave them each a present, which was to render
them charming in the eyes of their husbands, and secure the affection
of those gentlemen as long as they lived. What good did my Rose
and my Ring do these two women? None on earth. From having
all their whims indulged by their husbands, they became capricious,
lazy, ill-humored, absurdly vain, and leered and languished, and fan-
cied themselves irresistibly beautiful, when they were really quite old
and hideous, the ridiculous creatures! They used actually to patronize
me when I went to pay them a visit; *me*, the Fairy Blackstick, who
knows all the wisdom of the necromancers, and who could have turned them into baboons, and all their diamonds into strings of onions by
a single wave of my rod!" So she locked up her books in her cupboard, declined further magical performances, and scarcely used her
wand at all except as a cane to walk about with.

So when Duke Padella's lady had a little son (the duke was at that
time only one of the principal noblemen in Crim Tartary), Blackstick,
although invited to the christening, would not so much as attend, but
merely sent her compliments and a silver pap-boat for the baby, which
was really not worth a couple of guineas. About the same time the
Queen of Pallagonia presented his majesty with a son and heir; and
guns were fired, the capital illuminated, and no end of feasts ordained
to celebrate the young prince's birth. It was thought the fairy, who
was asked to be his godmother, would, at least, have presented him
with an invisible jacket, a flying horse, a Fortunatus's purse, or some
other valuable token of her favor; but instead, Blackstick went up to
the cradle of the child Giglio, when every body was admiring him
and complimenting his royal papa and mamma, and said, " My poor
child, the best thing I can send you is a little *misfortune*," and this
was all she would utter, to the disgust of Giglio's parents, who died

very soon after, when Giglio's uncle took the throne, as we read in Chapter I.

In like manner, when CAVOLFIORE, King of Crim Tartary, had a christening of his only child ROSALBA, the Fairy Blackstick, who had been invited, was not more gracious than in Prince Giglio's case. While every body was expatiating over the beauty of the darling child, and congratulating its parents, the Fairy Blackstick looked very sadly at the baby and its mother, and said, " My good woman" (for the fairy was very familiar, and no more minded a queen than a washerwoman) —" my good woman, these people who are following you will be the first to turn against you; and as for this little lady, the best thing I can wish her is a *little misfortune*." So she touched Rosalba with her black wand, looked severely at the courtiers, motioned the queen an adieu with her hand, and sailed slowly up into the air out of the window.

When she was gone, the court people, who had been awed and silent in her presence, began to speak. " What an odious fairy she is," they said ; " a pretty fairy, indeed ! Why, she went to the King of Paflagonia's christening, and pretended to do all sorts of things for that family ; and what has happened ? the prince, her godson, has been turned off his throne by his uncle. Would we allow our sweet princess to be deprived of her rights by any enemy ? Never, never, never, never !"

And they all shouted in a chorus, " Never, never, never, never !"

Now I should like to know, and how did these fine courtiers show their fidelity ? One of King Cavolfiore's vassals, the Duke Padella just mentioned, rebelled against the king, who went out to chastise his rebellious subject, " Any one rebel against our beloved and august monarch !" cried the courtiers ; " any one resist *him ?* Pooh ! He is invincible, irresistible. He will bring home Padella a prisoner, and tie him to a donkey's tail, and drive him round the town, saying, 'This is the way the Great Cavolfiore treats rebels.' "

The king went forth to vanquish Padella ; and the poor queen, who was a very timid, anxious creature, grew so frightened and ill, that, I am sorry to say, she died ; leaving injunctions with her ladies to take care of the dear little Rosalba. Of course they said they would. Of course they vowed they would rather die than any harm should happen to the princess. At first the "Crim Tartar Court Journal" stated that the king was obtaining great victories over the audacious rebel : then it was announced that the troops of the infamous Padella were in flight : then it was said that the royal army would soon come up with the enemy, and then—then the news came that King Cavolfiore was vanquished and slain by his majesty King Padella the First !

At this news, half the courtiers ran off to pay their duty to the conquering chief, and the other half ran away, laying hands on all the best articles in the palace, and poor little Rosalba was left there quite alone—quite alone ; and she toddled from one room to another, crying, "Countess ! duchess !" (only she said 'tounless, duttess,' not being able to speak plain), " bring me my mutton sop ; my royal highness hungry ! Tounless, duttess !" And she went from the private apartments into the throne-room, and nobody was there ; and thence into the ball-room, and nobody was there ; and thence into the pages' room, and nobody was there ; and she toddled down the great staircase into the hall, and nobody was there ; and the door was open, and she went into the court, and into the garden, and thence into the wilderness, and thence into the forest where the wild beasts live, and was never heard of any more !

A piece of her torn mantle and one of her shoes were found in the wood in the mouths of two lioness's cubs, whom KING PADELLA and a royal hunting party shot—for he was king now, and reigned over Crim Tartary. "So the poor little princess is done for," said he ; "well, what's done can't be helped. Gentlemen, let us go to lunch-con!" And one of the courtiers took up the shoe and put it in his pocket. And there was an end of Rosalba!

IV.

HOW BLACKSTICK WAS NOT ASKED TO THE PRINCESS ANGELICA'S CHRISTENING.

WHEN the Princess Angelica was born, her parents not only did not ask the Fairy Blackstick to the christening party, but gave orders to their porter absolutely to refuse her if she called. This porter's name was Gruffanuff, and he had been selected for the post by their royal highnesses because he was a very tall, fierce man, who could say "Not at home" to a tradesman or an unwelcome visitor with a rudeness which frightened most such persons away. He was the husband of that countess whose picture we have just seen, and as long as they were together they quarreled from morning till night. Now this fellow tried his rudeness once too often, as you shall hear; for the Fairy Blackstick coming to call upon the prince and princess, who were actually sitting at the open drawing-room window, Gruffanuff not only denied them, but made the most *odious vulgar sign* as he was going to slam the door in the fairy's face! "Git away, hold Black-stick!" said he. "I tell you, master and missis ain't at home to you;" and he was, as we have said, *going* to slam the door.

But the fairy, with her wand, prevented the door being shut; and Gruffanuff came out again in a fury, swearing in the most abominable way, and asking the fairy "whether she thought he was going to stay at that there door hall day."

"You *are* going to stay at that door all day and all night, and for many a long year," the fairy said, very majestically; and Gruffanuff, coming out of the door, straddling before it with his great calves, burst out laughing, and cried, "Ha, ha, ha! this *is* a good un! Ha—ah— what's this? Let me down—O—o—H'm!" and then he was dumb.

For, as the fairy waved her wand over him, he felt himself rising off the ground, and fluttering up against the door, and then, as if a screw ran into his stomach, he felt a dreadful pain there, and was pinned to the door; and then his arms flew up over his head; and his legs, after writhing about wildly, twisted under his body; and he felt cold, cold, growing over him, as if he was turning into metal, and he said, "O—o—H'm!" and could say no more, because he was dumb.

He *was* turned into metal! He was from being *brazen, brass!* He was neither more nor less than a knocker! And there he was, nailed to the door in the blazing summer day, till he burned almost red hot; and there he was, nailed to the door all the bitter winter nights, till his brass nose was dropping with icicles. And the postman came and

RING ALSO

rapped at him, and the vulgarest boy with a letter came and hit him up against the door. And the king and queen (princess and prince they were then) coming home from a walk that evening, the king said, "Hullo, my dear! you have had a new knocker put on the door. Why, it's rather like our porter in the face! What has become of that boozy vagabond?" And the housemaid came and scrubbed his nose with sandpaper; and once, when the Princess Angelica's little sister was born, he was tied up in an old kid glove; and, another night, some *larking* young men tried to wrench him off, and put him to the most excruciating agony with a turnscrew. And then the queen had a fancy to have the color of the door altered; and the painters dabbed him over the mouth and eyes, and nearly choked him, as they painted him pea-green. I warrant he had leisure to repent of having been rude to the Fairy Blackstick!

As for his wife, she did not miss him; and as he was always guzzling beer at the public house, and notoriously quarreling with his wife, and in debt to the tradesmen, it was supposed he had run away from all these evils, and emigrated to Australia or America. And when the prince and princess chose to become king and queen, they left their old house, and nobody thought of the porter any more.

V.

HOW PRINCESS ANGELICA TOOK A LITTLE MAID.

ONE day, when the Princess Angelica was quite a little girl, she was walking in the garden of the palace, with Mrs. Gruffanuff, the governess, holding a parasol over her head, to keep her sweet complexion from the freckles, and Angelica was carrying a bun, to feed the swans and ducks in the royal pond.

They had not reached the duck-pond, when there came toddling up to them such a funny little girl! She had a great quantity of hair blowing about her chubby little cheeks, and looked as if she had not been washed or combed for ever so long. She wore a ragged bit of a cloak, and had only one shoe on.

"You little wretch, who let you in here?" asked Gruffanuff.

"Dive me dat bun," said the little girl; "me vely hungry."

"Hungry! what is that?" asked Princess Angelica, and gave the child the bun.

"Oh, princess!" says Gruffanuff, "how good, how kind, how truly angelical you are! See, your majesties," she said to the king and queen, who now came up, along with their nephew, Prince Giglio, "how kind the princess is! She met this little dirty wretch in the garden—I can't tell how she came in here, or why the guards did not shoot her dead at the gate! and the dear darling of a princess has given her the whole of her bun!"

"I didn't want it," said Angelica.

"But you are a darling little angel all the same," says the governess.

"Yes, I know I am," said Angelica. "Dirty little girl, don't you think I am very pretty?" Indeed, she had on the finest of little dresses and hats; and, as her hair was carefully curled, she really looked very well.

"Oh, pooty, pooty!" says the little girl, capering about, laughing, and dancing, and munching her bun; and as she ate it she began to sing, "Oh what fun, to have a plum bun! how I wis it never was done!" At which, and her funny accent, Angelica, Giglio, and the king and queen began to laugh very merrily.

"I can dance as well as sing," says the little girl. "I can dance, and I can sing, and I can do all sorts of ting." And she ran to a flower-bed, and, pulling a few polyanthuses, rhododendrons, and other flowers made herself a little wreath, and danced before the king and queen so drolly and prettily, that every body was delighted.

"Who was your mother—who were your relations, little girl?" said the queen.

The little girl said, "Little lion was my brudder; great big lioness my mudder; neber heard of any udder." And she capered away on her one shoe, and every body was exceedingly diverted.

So Angelica said to the queen, "Mamma, my parrot flew away yesterday out of its cage, and I don't care any more for any of my toys; and I think this funny little dirty child will amuse me. I will take her home, and give her some of my old frocks—"

"Oh, the generous darling!" says Gruffanuff.

"Which I have worn ever so many times, and am quite tired of," Angelica went on; "and she shall be my little maid. Will you come home with me, little dirty girl?"

The child clapped her hands, and said, "Go home with you—yes! You pooty princess! Have a nice dinner, and wear a new dress!"

And they all laughed again, and took home the child to the palace, where, when she was washed and combed, and had one of the princess's frocks given to her, she looked as handsome as Angelica almost. Not that Angelica ever thought so; for this little lady never imagined that any body in the world could be as pretty, as good, or as clever as herself. In order that the little girl should not become too proud and conceited, Mrs. Gruffanuff took her old ragged mantle and one shoe, and put them into a glass box, with a card laid upon them, upon which was written, "These were the old clothes in which little BETSINDA was found, when the great goodness and admirable kindness of her royal highness the Princess Angelica received this little outcast." And the date was added, and the box locked up.

For a while little Betsinda was a great favorite with the princess, and she danced, and sang, and made her little rhymes, to amuse her mistress. But then the princess got a monkey, and afterward a little dog, and afterward a doll, and did not care for Betsinda any more, who became very melancholy and quiet, and sang no more funny songs, because nobody cared to hear her. And then, as she grew older, she was made a little lady's maid to the princess; and though she had no

wages, she worked, and mended, and put Angelica's hair in papers, and
was never cross when scolded, and was always eager to please her
mistress, and was always up early and to bed late, and at hand when
wanted, and, in fact, became a perfect little maid.   So the two girls
grew up, and, when the princess came out, Betsinda was never tired
of waiting on her, and made her dresses better than the best milliner,
and was useful in a hundred ways.   While the princess was having
her masters, Betsinda would sit and watch them, and in this way she
picked up a great deal of learning ; for she was always awake, though
her mistress was not, and listened to the wise professors when Angelica was yawning, or thinking of the next ball.   And when the dancing-
master came, Betsinda learned along with Angelica ; and when the
music-master came, she watched him, and practiced the princess's
pieces when Angelica was away at balls and parties ; and when the
drawing-master came, she took note of all he said and did ; and the
same with French, Italian, and all other languages—she learned them
from the teacher who came to Angelica.   When the princess was going out of an evening, she would say, " My good Betsinda, you may as
well finish what I have begun."   " Yes, miss," Betsinda would say, and
sit down very cheerful, not to *finish* what Angelica begun, but to *do* it.

For instance, the princess would begin the head of a warrior, let us
say, and when it was began it was something like this.

But when it was done, the warrior was like this

(only handsomer still, if possible), and the princess put her name to
the drawing; and the court, and king and queen, and, above all, poor
Giglio, admired the picture of all things, and said, " Was there ever a
genius like Angelica ?" So, I am sorry to say, was it with the princess's embroidery and other accomplishments : and Angelica actually
believed that she did these things herself, and received all the flattery
of the court as if every word of it was true.   Thus she began to think
that there was no young woman in all the world equal to herself, and
that no young man was good enough for her.   As for Betsinda, as she
heard none of these praises, she was not puffed up by them, and being
a most grateful, good-natured girl, she was only too anxious to do every
thing which might give her mistress pleasure.   Now you begin to perceive that Angelica had faults of her own, and was by no means such
a wonder of wonders as people represented her royal highness to be.

VI.

HOW PRINCE GIGLIO BEHAVED HIMSELF.

AND now let us speak about Prince Giglio, the nephew of the reigning monarch of Paflagonia. It has already been stated, in page 11, that as long as he had a smart coat to wear, a good horse to ride, and money in his pocket, or rather to take out of his pocket, for he was very good-natured, my young prince did not care for the loss of his crown and sceptre, being a thoughtless youth, not much inclined to politics or any kind of learning. So his tutor had a sinecure. Giglio would not learn classics or mathematics, and the lord chancellor of

Paflagonia, Squaretoso, pulled a very long face because the prince could not be got to study the Paflagonian laws and constitution ; but, on the other hand, the king's game-keepers and huntsmen found the prince an apt pupil ; the dancing-master pronounced that he was a most elegant and assiduous scholar : the first lord of the billiard table gave the most flattering reports of the prince's skill ; so did the groom of the tennis court ; and as for the captain of the guard and fencing-master, the *valiant* and *veteran* Count KUTASOFF HEDZOFF, he

avowed that since he ran the general of Crim Tartary, the dreadful Grumbuskin, through the body, he never had encountered so expert a swordsman as Prince Giglio.

C

I hope you do not imagine that there was any impropriety in the
prince and princess walking together in the palace garden, and because
Giglio kissed Angelica's hand in a polite manner.   In the first place,

they are cousins; next, the queen is walking in the garden too (you
can not see her, for she happens to be behind that tree), and her majesty always wished that Angelica and Giglio should marry: so did
Giglio : so did Angelica sometimes, for she thought her cousin very
handsome, brave, and good-natured ; but then, you know, she was so

clever, and knew so many things, and poor Giglio knew nothing, and
had no conversation. When they looked at the stars, what did Giglio
know of the heavenly bodies? Once when on a sweet night in a balcony where they were standing Angelica said, "There is the Bear,"
"Where?" says Giglio; "don't be afraid, Angelica! if a dozen bears
come, I will kill them rather than they shall hurt you." "Oh, you silly
creature!" says she, "you are very good, but you are not very wise."
When they looked at the flowers, Giglio was utterly unacquainted with
Botany, and had never heard of Linnæus. When the butterflies passed, Giglio knew nothing about them, being as ignorant of Entomology
as I am of Algebra. So, you see, Angelica, though she liked Giglio
pretty well, despised him on account of his ignorance. I think she
probably valued *her own learning* rather too much; but to think too well
of one's self is the fault of people of all ages and both sexes. Finally, when nobody else was there, Angelica liked her cousin well enough.

King Valoroso was very delicate in health, and, withal, so fond of good
dinners (which were prepared for him by his French cook, Marmitonio),

that it was supposed he could not live long. Now the idea of any
thing happening to the king struck the artful prime minister and the
designing old lady in waiting with terror; for, thought Glumboso
and the countess, " when Prince Giglio marries his cousin and comes
to the throne, what a pretty position we shall be in, whom he dis-
likes, and who have always been unkind to him. We shall lose our
places in a trice; Gruffanuff will have to give up all the jewels, laces,
snuff-boxes, rings, and watches which belonged to the queen, Giglio's
mother; and Glumboso will be forced to refund two hundred and
seventeen thousand million, nine hundred and eighty-seven thousand,
four hundred and thirty-nine pounds, thirteen shillings, and sixpence
halfpenny, money left to Prince Giglio by his poor dear father." So
the lady of honor and the prime minister hated Giglio because they
had done him a wrong; and these unprincipled people invented a
hundred cruel stories about poor Giglio, in order to influence the king,
queen, and princess against him; how he was so ignorant that he
could not spell the commonest words, and actually wrote Valoroso
Valloroso, and spelled Angelica with two l's; how he drank a great
deal too much wine at dinner, and was always idling in the stables
with the grooms; how he owed ever so much money at the pastry-
cook's and the haberdasher's; how he used to go to sleep at church;
how he was fond of playing cards with the pages. So did the queen
like playing cards; so did the king go to sleep at church, and eat
and drink too much; and, if Giglio owed a trifle for tarts, who owed
him two hundred and seventeen thousand million, nine hundred and
eighty-seven thousand, four hundred and thirty-nine pounds, thirteen
shillings, and sixpence halfpenny, I should like to know? Detract-
ors and tale-bearers (in my humble opinion) had much better look at
home. All this backbiting and slandering had effect upon Princess
Angelica, who began to look coldly on her cousin, then to laugh at
him and scorn him for being so stupid, then to sneer at him for having
vulgar associates; and at court balls, dinners, and so forth, to treat

him so unkindly that poor Giglio became quite ill, took to his bed, and sent for the doctor.

His majesty King Valoroso, as we have seen, had his own reasons for disliking his nephew; and as for those innocent readers who ask why, I beg (with the permission of their dear parents) to refer them to Shakspeare's pages, where they will read why King John disliked Prince Arthur. With the queen, his royal but weak-minded aunt, when Giglio was out of sight he was out of mind. While she had her whist and her evening parties, she cared for little else.

I dare say *two villains*, who shall be nameless, wished Doctor Pildrafto, the court physician, had killed Giglio right out; but he only bled and physicked him so severely, that the prince was kept to his room for several months, and grew as thin as a post.

While he was lying sick in this way, there came to the court of Paflagonia a famous painter, whose name was Tomaso Lorenzo, and who was painter in ordinary to the King of Crim Tartary, Paflagonia's neighbor.   Tomaso Lorenzo painted all the court, who were delighted with his works ; for even Countess Gruffanuff looked young and Ghumboso good-humored in his pictures.   " He flatters very much," some people said.   " Nay !" says Princess Angelica, " I am above flattery, and I think he did not make my picture handsome enough.   I can't bear to hear a man of genius unjustly cried down, and I hope my dear papa will make Lorenzo a knight of his Order of the Cucumber."

The Princess Angelica, although the courtiers vowed her royal highness could draw so *beautifully* that the idea of her taking lessons was absurd, yet chose to have Lorenzo for a teacher, and it was wonderful, *as long as she painted in his studio*, what beautiful pictures she made !   Some of the performances were engraved for the Book of Beauty ; others were sold for enormous sums at charity bazars.   She wrote the *signatures* under the drawings, no doubt, but I think I know who did the pictures—this artful painter, who had come with other designs on Angelica than merely to teach her to draw.

One day Lorenzo showed the princess a portrait of a young man in armor, with fair hair and the loveliest blue eyes, and an expression at once melancholy and interesting.

" Dear Signor Lorenzo, who is this ?" asked the princess.   " I never saw any one so handsome," says Countess Gruffanuff (the old humbug).

" That," said the painter, " that, madam, is the portrait of my august young master, His Royal Highness Bulbo, Crown Prince of Crim Tartary, Duke of Acroceraunia, Marquis of Poluphloisboio, and Knight Grand Cross of the Order of the Pumpkin.   That is the Order of the Pumpkin glittering on his manly breast, and received by his royal highness from his august father, his majesty King PADELLA I., for his gallantry at the battle of Rimbombamento, when he slew with his own princely hand the King of Ograria, and two hundred and eleven giants of the two hundred and eighteen who formed the king's body-guard.

The remainder were destroyed by the brave Crim Tartar army after an obstinate combat, in which the Crim Tartars suffered severely."

What a prince! thought Angelica; so brave—so calm-looking—so young—what a hero!

" He is as accomplished as he is brave," continued the court painter.

"He knows all languages perfectly; sings deliciously; plays every instrument; composes operas which have been acted a thousand nights running at the Imperial Theatre of Crim Tartary, and danced in a ballet there before the king and queen, in which he looked so beautiful, that his cousin, the lovely daughter of the King of Circassia, died for love of him."

"Why did he not marry the poor princess?" asked Angelica, with a sigh.

"Because they were *first cousins*, madam, and the clergy forbid these unions," said the painter. "And, besides, the young prince had given his royal heart *elsewhere*."

"And to whom?" asked her royal highness.

"I am not at liberty to mention the princess's name," answered the painter.

"But you may tell me the first letter of it," gasped out the princess.

"That your royal highness is at liberty to guess," says Lorenzo.

"Does it begin with a Z?" asked Angelica.

The painter said it wasn't a Z; then she tried a Y; then an X; then a W, and went so backward through almost the whole alphabet.

When she came to D, and it wasn't D, she grew very much excited; when she came to C, and it wasn't C, she was still more nervous; when she came to B, *and it wasn't B*, "O, dearest Gruffanuff," she said, "lend me your smelling bottle!" and, hiding her head on the countess's shoulder, she faintly whispered, "Ah, signor, can it be A?"

"It was A; and though I may not, by my royal master's orders, tell your royal highness the princess's name, whom he fondly, madly, devotedly, rapturously loves, I may show you her portrait," says this slyboots: and, leading the princess up to a gilt frame, he drew a curtain which was before it.

O goodness, the frame contained A LOOKING-GLASS! and Angelica saw her own face!

VII.

HOW GIGLIO AND ANGELICA HAD A QUARREL.

THE court painter of his majesty the King of Crim Tartary returned to that monarch's dominions, carrying away a number of sketches which he had made in the Paflagonian capital (you know, of course, my dears, that the name of that capital is Blombodinga); but the most charming of all his pieces was a portrait of the Princess Angelica, which all the Crim Tartar nobles came to see. With this work the king was so delighted, that he decorated the painter with his Order of the Pumpkin (sixth class), and the artist became Sir Tomaso Lorenzo, K.P., thenceforth.

King Valoroso also sent Sir Tomaso his Order of the Cucumber, besides a handsome order for money, for he painted the king, queen, and principal nobility while at Blombodinga, and became all the fashion, to the perfect rage of all the artists in Paflagonia, where the king used to point to the portrait of Prince Bulbo, which Sir Tomaso had left behind him, and say, " Which among you can paint a picture like that ?"

It hung in the royal parlor, over the royal sideboard, and Princess Angelica could always look at it as she sat making the tea. Each day it seemed to grow handsomer and handsomer, and the princess grew so fond of looking at it, that she would often spill the tea over the cloth, at which her father and mother would wink and wag their heads, and say to each other, " Aha ! we see how things are going."

In the mean while poor Giglio lay up stairs very sick in his chamber, though he took all the doctor's horrible medicines like a good young lad, as I hope *you* do, my dears, when you are ill, and mamma sends for the medical man. And the only person who visited Giglio (besides his friend the captain of the guard, who was almost always busy on parade), was little Betsinda, the housemaid, who used to do his bed-room and sitting-room out, bring him his gruel, and warm his bed.

When the little housemaid came to him in the morning and evening, Prince Giglio used to say, "Betsinda, Betsinda, how is the Princess Angelica?"

And Betsinda used to answer, "The princess is very well, thank you, my lord." And Giglio would heave a sigh, and think, if Angelica were sick, I am sure *I* should not be very well.

Then Giglio would say, "Betsinda, has the Princess Angelica asked for me to-day?" And Betsinda would answer, "No, my lord, not to-day;" or, "She was very busy practicing the piano when I saw her;" or, "She was writing invitations for an evening party, and did not speak to me;" or make some excuse or other not strictly consonant with truth; for Betsinda was such a good-natured creature, that she strove to do every thing to prevent annoyance to Prince Giglio, and even brought him up roast chicken and jellies from the kitchen (when the doctor allowed them, and Giglio was getting better), saying "that the princess had made the jelly or the bread-sauce with her own hands, on purpose for Giglio."

When Giglio heard this, he took heart, and began to mend immediately, and gobbled up all the jelly, and picked the last bone of the chicken — drumsticks, merry-thought, side-bones, back, pope's nose, and all—thanking his dear Angelica; and he felt so much better the next day, that he dressed and went down stairs, where, whom should he meet but Angelica going into the drawing-room. All the covers were off the chairs, the chandeliers were taken out of the bags, the damask curtains uncovered, the work and things carried away, and the

handsomest albums on the tables.   Angelica had her hair in papers;
in a word, it was evident there was going to be a party.

" Heavens, Giglio!" cries Angelica; "*you* here, in such a dress!   What
a figure you are !"

" Yes, dear Angelica, I am come down stairs, and feel so well to-day,
thanks to the *fowl* and the *jelly*."

" What do I know about fowls and jellies, that you allude to them
in that rude way ?" says Angelica.

" Why, didn't—didn't you send them, Angelica, dear ?" says Giglio.

" I send them, indeed ! Angelica dear !   No, Giglio, dear," says she,
mocking him, "*I* was engaged in getting the rooms ready for his royal
highness the Prince of Crim Tartary, who is coming to pay my papa's
court a visit."

" The—Prince—of—Crim—Tartary !" Giglio said, aghast.

" Yes, the Prince of Crim Tartary," says Angelica, mocking him.   " I
dare say you never heard of such a country.   What *did* you ever hear
of ?   You don't know whether Crim Tartary is on the Red Sea or on
the Black Sea, I dare say."

" Yes I do; it's on the Red Sea," says Giglio, at which the princess
burst out laughing at him, and said, " O you ninny !   You are so ignorant, you are really not fit for society !   You know nothing but about
horses and dogs, and are only fit to dine in a mess-room with my royal
father's heaviest dragoons.   Don't look so surprised at me, sir; go and
put your best clothes on to receive the prince, and let me get the drawing-room ready."

Giglio said, " O Angelica, Angelica, I didn't think this of you.   *This*
wasn't your language to me when you gave me this ring, and I gave
you mine in the garden, and you gave me that k—"

But what k was we never shall know, for Angelica, in a rage, cried,
" Get out, you saucy, rude creature !   How dare you to remind me of
your rudeness ?   As for your little trumpery twopenny ring, there, sir,
there !"   And she flung it out of the window.

"It was my mother's marriage ring," cried Giglio.

"*I* don't care whose marriage ring it was," cries Angelica. "Marry the person who picks it up, if she's a woman: you sha'n't marry *me*. And give me back *my* ring. I've no patience with people who boast about the things they give away! *I* know who'll give me much finer things than you ever gave me. A beggarly ring indeed, not worth five shillings!"

Now Angelica little knew that the ring which Giglio had given her was a fairy ring: if a man wore it, it made all the women in love with him; if a woman, all the gentlemen. The queen, Giglio's mother, quite an ordinary looking person, was admired immensely while she wore this ring, and her husband was frantic when she was ill. But when she called her little Giglio to her, and put the ring on his finger, King Savio did not seem to care for his wife so much any more, but transferred all his love to little Giglio. So did every body love him as long as he had the ring; but when, as quite a child, he gave it to Angelica, people began to love and admire *her;* and Giglio, as the saying is, played only second fiddle.

"Yes," says Angelica, going on in her foolish, ungrateful way, "*I* know who'll give me much finer things than your beggarly little pearl nonsense."

"Very good, miss! You may take back your ring too!" says Giglio, his eyes flashing fire at her; and then, as if his eyes had been suddenly opened, he cried out, "Ha! what does this mean? Is *this* the woman I have been in love with all my life? Have I been such a ninny as to throw away my regard upon *you?* Why—actually—yes—you are a little crooked!"

"O you wretch!" cries Angelica.

"And, upon my conscience, you—you squint a little."

"E!" cries Angelica.

"And your hair is red—and you are marked with the small-pox—and what? you have three false teeth—and one leg shorter than the other!"

"You brute, you brute, you!" Angelica screamed out: and as she seized the ring with one hand, she dealt Giglio one, two, three smacks on the face, and would have pulled the hair off his head had he not started laughing, and crying,

"O dear me, Angelica, don't pull out *my* hair, it hurts! You might remove a great deal of *your own*, as I perceive, without scissors or pulling at all. O ho, ho! ha, ha, ha! he, he, he!"

And he nearly choked himself with laughing, and she with rage, when, with a low bow, and dressed in his court habit, Count Gambabella, the first lord in waiting, entered and said, "Royal highnesses! their majesties expect you in the pink throne-room, where they await the arrival of the Prince of CRIM TARTARY."

VIII.

HOW GRUFFANUFF PICKED THE FAIRY RING UP, AND PRINCE BULBO CAME TO COURT.

PRINCE BULBO's arrival had set all the court in a flutter: every body was ordered to put his or her best clothes on: the footmen had their gala liveries: the lord chancellor his new wig; the guards their last new tunics; and Countess Gruffanuff, you may be sure, was glad of an opportunity of decorating her old person with her finest things. She was walking through the court of the palace, on her way to wait upon their majesties, when she spied something glittering on the pavement, and bade the boy in buttons, who was holding up her train, to go and pick up the article shining yonder. He was an ugly little wretch, in some of the groom-porter's old clothes cut down, and much too tight for him; and yet, when he had taken up the ring (as it turned out to be), and was carrying it to his mistress, she thought he looked like a little cupid. He gave the ring to her; it was a trumpery little thing enough, but too small for any of her old knuckles, so she put it into her pocket.

"O mum!" says the boy, looking at her, "how, how beyoutiful you do look, mum, to-day, mum!"

"And you too, Jacky," she was going to say; but, looking down at him—no, he was no longer good-looking at all—but only the carroty-

haired little Jacky of the morning.   However, praise is welcome from
the ugliest of men or boys, and Gruffanuff, bidding the boy hold up

her train, walked on in high good-humor.   The guards saluted her
with peculiar respect.   Captain Hedzoff, in the ante-room, said, " My
dear madam, you look like an angel to-day."   And so, bowing and
smirking, Gruffanuff went in and took her place behind her royal mas-

HIS R. H. THE PRINCE OF CRIM TARTARY.

ter and mistress, who were in the throne-room, awaiting the Prince of
Crim Tartary. Princess Angelica sat at their feet, and behind the
king's chair stood Prince Giglio, looking very savage.

The Prince of Crim Tartary made his appearance, attended by Baron
Sleibootz, his chamberlain, and followed by a black page, carrying the
most beautiful crown you ever saw. He was dressed in his traveling
costume, and his hair, as you see, was a little in disorder. " I have
ridden three hundred miles since breakfast," said he, " so eager was I
to behold the Prin—the court and august family of Paflagonia—and I
could not wait one minute before appearing in your majesties' pres-
ences."

Giglio, from behind the throne, burst out into a roar of contemptu-
ous laughter; but all the royal party, in fact, were so flurried that they
did not hear this outbreak. " Your royal highness is welcome in
any dress," says the king. " Glumboso, a chair for his royal highness."

" Any dress his royal highness wears *is* a court dress," says Princess
Angelica, smiling graciously.

" Ah! but you should see my other clothes," said the prince. " I
should have had them on, but that stupid carrier has not brought
them. Who's that laughing?"

It was Giglio laughing. " I was laughing," he said, " because you
said just now that you were in such a hurry to see the princess, that
you could not wait to change your dress; and now you say you come
in those clothes because you have no others."

" And who are you?" said Prince Bulbo, very fiercely.

" My father was king of this country, and I am his only son, prince,"
replies Giglio, with equal haughtiness.

" Ha!" said the king and Glumboso, looking very flurried; but the
former, collecting himself, said, " Dear Prince Bulbo, I forgot to intro-
duce to your royal highness my dear nephew, his royal highness
Prince Giglio! Know each other! embrace each other! Giglio,

give his royal highness your hand!" and Giglio, giving his hand,
squeezed poor Bulbo's until the tears ran out of his eyes. Glumboso
now brought a chair for the royal visitor, and placed it on the platform
on which the king, queen, and prince were seated; but the chair was
on the edge of the platform, and as Bulbo sat down, it toppled over,
and he with it, rolling over and over, and bellowing like a bull.
Giglio roared still louder at this disaster, but it was with laughter;
so did all the court, when Prince Bulbo got up; for though, when
he entered the room, he appeared not very ridiculous, as he stood up
from his fall for a moment, he looked so exceedingly plain and foolish,
that nobody could help laughing at him. When he had entered the
room, he was observed to carry a rose in his hand, which fell out of it
as he tumbled.

"My rose! my rose!" cried Bulbo; and his chamberlain dashed forward and picked it up, and gave it to the prince, who put it into his
waistcoat. Then people wondered why they had laughed—there was
nothing particularly ridiculous in him. He was rather short, rather
stout, rather red-haired; but, in fine, for a prince, not so bad.

So they sat and talked—the royal personages together, the Crim Tartar officers with those of Paflagonia—Giglio very comfortable with
Gruffanuff behind the throne. He looked at her with such tender eyes,
that her heart was all in a flutter. "Oh, dear prince," said she, "how
could you speak so haughtily in presence of their majesties? I pro-
test I thought I should have fainted."

"I should have caught you in my arms," said Giglio, looking rap-
tures.

"Why were you so cruel to Prince Bulbo, dear prince?" says Gruff.
"Because I hate him," says Gil.

"You are jealous of him, and still love poor Angelica," cries Gruffanuff, putting her handkerchief to her eyes.

"I did, but I love her no more!" Giglio cried. "I despise her!
Were she heiress to twenty thousand thrones, I would despise her and

scorn her. But why speak of thrones? I have lost mine. I am too
weak to recover it—I am alone, and have no friend."

"Oh, say not so, dear prince!" says Gruffanuff.

"Besides," says he, "I am so happy here *behind the throne* that I
would not change my place, no, not for the throne of the world!"

"What are you two people chattering about there?" says the queen,
who was rather good-natured, though not overburdened with wisdom.
"It is time to dress for dinner. Giglio, show Prince Bulbo to his room.
Prince, if your clothes have not come, we shall be very happy to see
you as you are." But when Prince Bulbo got to his bed-room, his
luggage was there and unpacked; and the hair-dresser coming in, cut
and curled him entirely to his own satisfaction; and when the dinner-

bell rang, the royal company had not to wait above five-and-twenty minutes until Bulbo appeared, during which time the king, who could not bear to wait, grew as sulky as possible. As for Giglio, he never left Madam Gruffanuff all this time, but stood with her in the embrasure of a window, paying her compliments. At length the groom of the chambers announced his royal highness the Prince of Crim Tartary! and the noble company went into the royal dining-room. It was quite a small party—only the king and queen, the princess, whom Bulbo took out, the two princes, Countess Gruffanuff, Glumboso, the prime minister, and Prince Bulbo's chamberlain. You may be sure they had a very good dinner: let every boy or girl think of what she likes best, and fancy it on the table.*

The princess talked incessantly all dinner time to the Prince of Crimea, who ate an immense deal too much, and never took his eyes off his plate, except when Giglio, who was carving a goose, sent a quantity of stuffing and onion sauce into one of them. Giglio only burst out a laughing as the Crimean prince wiped his shirt-front and face with his scented pocket-handkerchief. He did not make Prince Bulbo any apology. When the prince looked at him, Giglio would not look that way. When Prince Bulbo said, " Prince Giglio, may I have the honor of taking a glass of wine with you?" Giglio *wouldn't* answer. All his talk and his eyes were for Countess Gruffanuff, who, you may be sure, was pleased with Giglio's attentions—the vain old creature! When he was not complimenting her, he was making fun of Prince Bulbo, so loud that Gruffanuff was always tapping him with her fan, and saying, "O you satirical prince! O fy, the prince will hear!" " Well, I don't mind," says Giglio, louder still. The king and queen luckily did not hear; for her majesty was a little deaf, and the king thought so much about his own dinner, and, besides, made such a dreadful noise hobgobbling in eating it, that he heard nothing else. After dinner, his majesty and the queen went to sleep in their arm-chairs.

This was the time when Giglio began his tricks with Prince Bulbo, plying that young gentleman with Port, Sherry, Madeira, Champagne, Marsala, Cherry Brandy, and pale Ale, of all of which Master Bulbo drank without stint. But, in plying his guest, Giglio was obliged to

* Here a very pretty game may be played by all the children saying what they like best for dinner.

drink himself, and, I am sorry to say, took more than was good for him,
so that the young men were very noisy, rude, and foolish when they
joined the ladies after dinner; and dearly did they pay for that im-
prudence, as now, my darlings, you shall hear.

Bulbo went and sat by the piano, where Angelica was playing and
singing, and he sang out of tune, and he upset the coffee when the
footman brought it, and he laughed out of place, and talked absurdly, and fell asleep, and snored horridly. Booh, the nasty pig! But,
as he lay there, stretched on the pink satin sofa, Angelica still per-
sisted in thinking him the most beautiful of human beings. No doubt
the magic rose which Bulbo wore caused this infatuation on Angelica's
part; but is she the first young woman who has thought a silly fellow
charming?

Giglio must go and sit by Gruffanuff, whose old face he, too, every
moment began to find more lovely. He paid the most outrageous
compliments to her. There never was such a darling—Older than he
was? Fiddle-de-dee! He would marry her—he would have nothing
but her!

To marry the heir to the throne! Here was a chance! The artful
hussy actually got a sheet of paper, and wrote upon it, " This is to
give notice that I, Giglio, only son of Savio, King of Paflagonia, hereby
promise to marry the charming and virtuous Barbara Griselda Countess Gruffanuff, and widow of the late Jenkins Gruffanuff, Esq."

" What is it you are writing, you charming Gruffy?" says Giglio,
who was lolling on the sofa, by the writing-table.

" Only an order for you to sign, dear prince, for giving coals and
blankets to the poor this cold weather. Look, the king and queen are
both asleep, and your royal highness's order will do."

So Giglio, who was very good-natured, as Gruffy well knew, signed
the order immediately; and, when she had it in her pocket, you may
fancy what airs she gave herself. She was ready to flounce out of the
room before the queen herself, as now she was the wife of the *right-*

ful King of Paflagonia! She would not speak to Glumboso, whom she thought a brute, for depriving her *dear husband* of the crown! And when candles came, and she had helped to undress the queen and

princess, she went into her own room, and actually practiced, on a sheet of paper, "Griselda Paflagonia," "Barbara Regina," "Grizelda Barbara, Paf. Reg.," and I don't know what signatures besides, against the day when she should be queen, forsooth!

IX.

HOW BETSINDA GOT THE WARMING-PAN.

LITTLE Betsinda came in to put Gruffanuff's hair in papers, and the countess was so pleased, that, for a wonder, she complimented Betsinda. " Betsinda," she said, " you dressed my hair very nicely to-day ; I promised you a little present. Here are five sh— No, here is a pretty little ring that I picked—that I have had some time." And she gave Betsinda the ring she had picked up in the court. It fitted Betsinda exactly

" It's like the ring the princess used to wear," says the maid.

" No such thing," says Gruffanuff ; " I have had it this ever so long. There—tuck me up quite comfortable. And now, as it's a very cold night" (the snow was beating in at the window), " you may go and warm dear Prince Giglio's bed, like a good girl, and then you may un-rip my green silk, and then you can just do me up a little cap for the morning, and then you can mend that hole in my silk stocking, and then you can go to bed, Betsinda. Mind, I shall want my cup of tea at five o'clock in the morning."

" I suppose I had best warm both the young gentlemen's beds, ma'am," says Betsinda.

Gruffanuff, for reply, said, " Hau-au-ho !—Grau-haw-hoo !—Hong hrho !" In fact, she was snoring sound asleep.

Her room, you know, is next to the king and queen, and the princess's is next to them. So pretty Betsinda went away for the coals to the kitchen, and filled the royal warming-pan.

Now she was a very kind, merry, civil, pretty girl ; but there must have been something very captivating about her this evening, for all the women in the servants' hall began to scold and abuse her. The housekeeper said she was a pert, stuck-up thing; the upper house-maid asked how dare she wear such ringlets and ribbons, it was quite improper! The cook (for there was a woman cook as well as a man cook) said to the kitchen-maid that *she* never could see any thing in that creetur; but as for the men, every one of them, coachman, John, Buttons the page, and Monsieur, the Prince of Crim Tartary's valet, started up, and said,

" My eyes!
" O mussey!   } What a pretty girl Betsinda is."
" O jemmany!
" O ciel!

" Hands off; none of your impertinence, you vulgar, low people!" says Betsinda, walking off with her pan of coals. She heard the young gentlemen playing at billiards as she went up stairs; first to Prince Giglio's bed, which she warmed, and then to Prince Bulbo's room.

He came in just as she had done, and as soon as he saw her, " O! O! O! O! O! O! what a beyou—oo—ootiful creature you are. You angel—you peri—you rose-bud, let me be thy bulbul—thy Bulbo too! Fly to the desert, fly with me! I never saw a young gazelle to glad me with its dark blue eye that had eyes like thine. Thou nymph of beauty, take, take this young heart. A truer never did itself sustain within a soldier's waistcoat. Be mine! Be mine! Be Princess of Crim Tartary! My royal father will approve our union : and as for that little carroty-haired Angelica, I do not care a fig for her any more."

" Go away, your royal highness, and go to bed, please," said Bet-sinda, with the warming-pan.

But Bulbo said, " No, never, till thou swearest to be mine, thou love-ly, blushing, chamber-maid divine! Here, at thy feet, the royal Bul-bo lies, the trembling captive of Betsinda's eyes."

And he went on, making himself so *absurd and ridiculous*, that Betsinda, who was full of fun, gave him a touch with the warming-pan, which, I promise you, made him cry "O-o-o-o!" in a very different manner.

Prince Bulbo made such a noise that Prince Giglio, who heard him from the next room, came in to see what was the matter. As soon as he saw what was taking place, Giglio, in a fury, rushed on Bulbo, kicked him in the rudest manner up to the ceiling, and went on kicking him till his hair was quite out of curl.

Poor Betsinda did not know whether to laugh or to cry; the kicking

THE RIVALS.

certainly must hurt the prince, but then he looked so droll! When
Giglio had done knocking him up and down to the ground, and while
he went into a corner rubbing himself, what do you think Giglio does?
He goes down on his own knees to Betsinda, takes her hand, begs her
to accept his heart, and offers to marry her that moment. Fancy Betsinda's condition, who had been in love with the prince ever since she
first saw him in the palace garden, when she was quite a little child.

"Oh, divine Betsinda!" says the prince, "how have I lived fifteen
years in thy company without seeing thy perfections? What woman
in all Europe, Asia, Africa, and America—nay, in Australia, only it is
not yet discovered, can presume to be thy equal? Angelica? Pish!
Gruffanuff? Phoo! The queen? Ha, ha! Thou art my queen. Thou
art the real Angelica, because thou art really angelic."

"Oh, prince! I am but a poor chambermaid," says Betsinda, looking, however, very much pleased.

"Didst thou not tend me in my sickness, when all forsook me?" continues Giglio. "Did not thy gentle hand smooth my pillow, and bring
me jelly and roast chicken?"

"Yes, dear prince, I did," says Betsinda, "and I sewed your royal
highness's shirt-buttons on too, if you please, your royal highness,"
cries this artless maiden.

When poor Prince Bulbo, who was now madly in love with Betsinda, heard this declaration, when he saw the unmistakable glances
which she flung upon Giglio, Bulbo began to cry bitterly, and tore
quantities of hair out of his head, till it all covered the room like so
much tow.

Betsinda had left the warming-pan on the floor while the princes
were going on with their conversation, and as they began now to quar-
rel and be very fierce with one another, she thought proper to run away.

"You great big blubbering booby, tearing your hair in the corner
there; of course you will give me satisfaction for insulting Betsinda.
You dare to kneel down at Princess Giglio's knees and kiss her hand!"

" She's not Princess Giglio!" roars out Bulbo.   " She shall be Princess Bulbo—no other shall be Princess Bulbo."

" You are engaged to my cousin!" bellows out Giglio.

" I hate your cousin," says Bulbo.

" You shall give me satisfaction for insulting her!" cries Giglio, in
a fury.

" I'll have your life."

" I'll run you through."

" I'll cut your throat."

" I'll blow your brains out."

" I'll knock your head off."

" I'll send a friend to you in the morning."

" I'll send a bullet into you in the afternoon."

" We'll meet again," says Giglio, shaking his fist in Bulbo's face,
and seizing up the warming-pan, he kissed it, because, forsooth, Betsinda had carried it, and rushed down stairs.   What should he see on
the landing but his majesty talking to Betsinda, whom he called by all
sorts of fond names.   His majesty had heard a row in the building, so
he stated, and smelling something burning, had come out to see what
the matter was.

" It's the young gentlemen smoking, perhaps, sir," says Betsinda.

" Charming chambermaid," says the king (like all the rest of them),
" never mind the young men!   Turn thy eyes on a middle-aged autocrat, who has been considered not ill-looking in his time."

" Oh, sir! what will her majesty say?" cries Betsinda.

" Her majesty!" laughs the monarch.   " Her majesty be hanged!
Am I not autocrat of Paflagonia?   Have I not blocks, ropes, axes, hang-
men—ha?   Runs not a river by my palace wall?   Have I not sacks
to sew up wives withal?   Say but the word, that thou wilt be mine
own—your mistress straightway in a sack is sewn, and thou the sharer
of my heart and throne."

When Giglio heard these atrocious sentiments, he forgot the respect usually paid to royalty, lifted up the warming-pan, and knocked down

the king as flat as a pancake; after which, Master Giglio took to his heels and ran away, and Betsinda went off screaming, and the queen, Grufanuff, and the princess all came out of their rooms. Fancy their feelings on beholding their husband, father, sovereign in this posture!

E

X.

HOW KING VALOROSO WAS IN A DREADFUL PASSION.

As soon as the coals began to burn him, the king came to himself and stood up. "Ho! my captain of the guards!" his majesty exclaimed, stamping his royal feet with rage. O piteous spectacle! the king's nose was bent quite crooked by the blow of Prince Giglio! His majesty

ground his teeth with rage. "Hedzoff," he said, taking a death-war-rant out of his dressing-gown pocket, "Hedzoff, good Hedzoff, seize upon the prince. Thou'lt find him in his chamber two pair up. But now he dared, with sacrilegious hand, to strike the sacred night-cap of a king, and floor me with a warming-pan! Away, no more demur; the villain dies! See it be done, or else—h'm!—ha!—h'm! mind thine own eyes!" and followed by the ladies, and lifting up the tails of his dressing-gown, the king entered his own apartment.

Captain Hedzoff was very much affected, having a sincere love for Giglio. "Poor, poor Giglio!" he said, the tears rolling over his manly face and dripping down his mustaches; "my noble young prince, is it my hand must lead thee to death?"

"Lead him to fiddlestick, Hedzoff," said a female voice. It was Gruffanuff, who had come out in her dressing-gown when she heard the noise. "The king said you were to hang the prince. Well, hang the prince."

"I don't understand you," says Hedzoff, who was not a very clever man.

"You gaby! he didn't say *which* prince," says Gruffanuff.

"No, he didn't say which, certainly," said Hedzoff.

"Well, then, take Bulbo, and hang *him!*"

When Captain Hedzoff heard this, he began to dance about for joy. "Obedience is a soldier's honor," says he. "Prince Bulbo's head will do capitally;" and he went to arrest the prince the very first thing next morning.

He knocked at the door. "Who's there?" says Bulbo. "Captain Hedzoff? Step in, pray, my good captain; I'm delighted to see you: I have been expecting you."

"Have you?" says Hedzoff.

"Sleibootz, my chamberlain, will act for me," says the prince.

"I beg your royal highness's pardon, but you will have to act for yourself, and it's a pity to wake Baron Sleibootz."

The Prince Bulbo still seemed to take the matter very coolly. "Of course, captain," says he, "you are come about that affair with Prince Giglio?"

"Precisely," says Hedzoff, "that affair of Prince Giglio."

"Is it to be pistols or swords, captain?" asked Bulbo. "I'm a pretty good hand with both; and I'll do for Prince Giglio, as sure as my name is my royal highness Prince Bulbo."

"There's some mistake, my lord," says the captain; "the business is done with *axes* among us."

"Axes? That's sharp work," says Bulbo. "Call my chamberlain; he'll be my second; and in ten minutes I flatter myself you'll see Master Giglio's head off his impertinent shoulders. I'm hungry for his blood. Hoo-oo, aw!" and he looked as savage as an ogre.

"I beg your pardon, sir, but by this warrant I am to take you prisoner, and hand you over to—to the executioner."

"Pooh! pooh! my good man! Stop, I say. Ho! hulloa!" was all that this luckless prince was enabled to say; for Hedzoff's guards, seizing him, tied a handkerchief over his mouth and face, and carried him to the place of execution.

The king, who happened to be talking to Glumboso, saw him pass.

and took a pinch of snuff, and said, " So much for Giglio!   Now let's
go to breakfast."

The captain of the guard handed over his prisoner to the sheriff,
with the fatal order,

"AT SIGHT, CUT OFF THE BEARER'S HEAD.
"VALOROSO XXIV."

" It's a mistake," says Bulbo, who did not seem to understand the
business in the least.

" Poo—poo—pooh!" says the sheriff.   " Fetch Jack Ketch instantly.
Jack Ketch!"

And poor Bulbo was led to the scaffold, where an executioner with
a block and a tremendous axe was always ready in case he should be
wanted.

But we must now revert to Giglio and Betsinda.

XI.

WHAT GRUFFANUFF DID TO GIGLIO AND BETSINDA.

GRUFFANUFF, who had seen what had happened with the king, and knew that Giglio must come to grief, got up very early the next morning, and went to devise some plans for rescuing her darling husband, as the silly old thing insisted on calling him. She found him walking up and down the garden, thinking of a rhyme for Betsinda (*tinder* and *winda* were all he could find), and, indeed, having forgotten all about the past evening, except that Betsinda was the most lovely of beings.

"Well, dear Giglio," says Gruff.

"Well, dear Gruffy," says Giglio, only *he* was quite satirical.

"I have been thinking, darling, what you must do in this scrape. You must fly the country for a while."

"What scrape?—fly the country? Never, without her I love, countess," says Giglio.

"No, she will accompany you, dear prince," she says, in her most coaxing accents. "First, we must get the jewels belonging to our royal parents, and those of her and his present majesty. Here is the key, duck; they are all yours, you know, by right; for you are the rightful King of Paflagonia, and your wife will be the rightful queen."

"Will she?" says Giglio.

"Yes; and, having got the jewels, go to Glumboso's apartment, where, under his bed, you will find sacks containing money to the amount of £217,000,987,139 13s. 6½d., all belonging to you, for he took it out of your royal father's room on the day of his death. With this we will fly."

"*We* will fly?" says Giglio.

"Yes, you and your bride—your affianced love—your Gruffy!" says the countess, with a languishing leer.

"*You*, my bride!" says Giglio. "You, you hideous old woman!"

"Oh, you, you wretch! didn't you give me this paper, promising marriage?" cries Gruff.

"Get away, you old goose! I love Betsinda, and Betsinda only!" And, in a fit of terror, he ran from her as quickly as he could.

"He! he! he!" shrieks out Gruff; "a promise is a promise, if there are laws in Paflagonia! And as for that monster, that wretch, that fiend, that ugly little vixen—as for that upstart, that ingrate, that beast, Betsinda, Master Giglio will have no little difficulty in discovering her whereabouts. He may look very long before finding *her*, I warrant. He little knows that Miss Betsinda is—"

Is—what? Now you shall hear. Poor Betsinda got up at five in a winter morning to bring her cruel mistress her tea, and, instead of finding her in a good humor, found Gruffy as cross as two sticks. The countess boxed Betsinda's ears half a dozen times while she was dressing; but, as poor little Betsinda was used to this kind of treatment, she did not feel any special alarm. "And now," says she, "when her majesty rings her bell twice, I'll trouble you, miss, to attend."

So, when the queen's bell rang twice, Betsinda came to her majesty and made a pretty little courtesy. The queen, the princess, and Gruffanuff were all three in the room. As soon as they saw her they began,

"You wretch!" says the queen.

"You little vulgar thing!" said the princess.

"You beast!" says Gruffanuff.

"Get out of my sight!" says the queen.

"Go away with you, do!" says the princess.

"Quit the premises!" says Gruffanuff.

Alas! and wo is me! very lamentable events had occurred to Betsinda that morning, and all in consequence of that fatal warming-pan business of the previous night. The king had offered to marry her; of course her majesty the queen was jealous: Bulbo had fallen in love with her; of course Angelica was furious: Giglio was in love with her, and oh what a fury Gruffy was in!

"Take off that { cap   } I gave you," they said, all at once, and
               { petticoat } began tearing the clothes off poor Bet-
               { gown   } sinda.

"How dare you { the king ?"   } cried the queen, the princess,
 flirt with   { Prince Bulbo ?" }   and countess.
               { Prince Giglio ?" }

"Give her the rags she wore when she came into the house, and turn her out of it!" cries the queen.

"Mind she does not go with *my* shoes on, which I lent her so kindly," says the princess; and, indeed, the princess's shoes were a great deal too big for Betsinda.

"Come with me, you filthy hussy!" and, taking up the queen's poker, the cruel Gruffanuff drove Betsinda into her room.

The countess went to the glass box in which she had kept Betsinda's old cloak and shoe this ever so long, and said, "Take those rags, you little beggar creature, and strip off every thing belonging to honest people, and go about your business;" and she actually tore off the poor little delicate thing's back almost all her things, and told her to be off out of the house.

Poor Betsinda huddled the cloak round her back, on which were embroidered the letters PRIN .... ROSAL .... and then came a great rent.

As for the shoe, what was she to do with one poor little tootsey sandal? The string was still to it, so she hung it round her neck.

"Won't you give me a pair of shoes to go out in the snow, mum, if you please, mum?" cried the poor child.

"No, you wicked beast!" says Gruffanuff, driving her along with the poker—driving her down the cold stairs—driving her through the cold hall—flinging her out into the cold street, so that the knocker itself shed tears to see her!

But a kind fairy made the soft snow warm for her little feet, and she wrapped herself up in the ermine of her mantle and was gone'

"And now let us think about breakfast," says the greedy queen.

"What dress shall I put on, mamma—the pink or the pea-green?" says Angelica. "Which do you think the dear prince will like best?"

"Mrs. V.!" sings out the king from his dressing-room, "Let us have sausages for breakfast! Remember, we have Prince Bulbo staying with us!"

And they all went to get ready.

Nine o'clock came, and they were all in the breakfast-room, and no Prince Bulbo as yet. The urn was hissing and humming; the muffins were smoking—such a heap of muffins! the eggs were done; there was a pot of raspberry jam, and coffee, and a beautiful chicken and tongue on the side-table. Marmitonio the cook brought in the sausages. O how nice they smelled!

"Where is Bulbo?" said the king. "John, where is his royal highness?"

John said he had a took hup his roilighnessesses shaving-water, and his clothes and things, and he wasn't in his room, which he sposed his royliness was just stepped hout.

"Stepped out before breakfast in the snow! Impossible!" says the king, sticking his fork into a sausage. "My dear, take one. Angelica, won't you have a saveloy?" The princess took one, being very fond of them; and at this moment Glumboso entered with Captain Hedzoff, both looking very much disturbed. "I am afraid your majesty—" cries Glumboso. "No business before breakfast, Glum!" says the king. "Breakfast first, business next. Mrs. V., some more sugar!"

"Sire, I am afraid if we wait till after breakfast it will be too late," says Glumboso. "He—he—he'll be hanged at half past nine."

"Don't talk about hanging and spoil my breakfast, you unkind, vulgar man you," cries the princess. "John, some mustard. Pray who is to be hanged?"

"Sire, it is the prince," whispers Glumboso to the king.

"Talk about business after breakfast, I tell you!" says his majesty, quite sulky.

"We shall have a war, sire, depend on it," says the minister. "His father, King Padella . . ."

"His father, King *who*?" says the king. "King Padella is not Giglio's father. My brother, King Savio, was Giglio's father."

"It's Prince Bulbo they are hanging, sire, not Prince Giglio," said the prime minister.

"You told me to hang the prince, and I took the ugly one," says Hedzoff. "I didn't, of course, think your majesty intended to murder your own flesh and blood!"

The king for all reply flung the plate of sausages at Hedzoff's head. The princess cried out "Hee-karee-karee!" and fell down in a fainting-fit.

"Turn the cock of the urn upon her royal highness," said the king, and the boiling water gradually revived her. His majesty looked at his watch, compared it by the clock in the parlor, and by that of the church in the square opposite; then he wound it up; then he looked at it again. "The great question is," says he, "am I fast or am I slow? If I am slow, we may as well go on with breakfast. If I'm fast, why there is just the possibility of saving Prince Bulbo. It's a doosid awkward mistake, and, upon my word, Hedzoff, I have the greatest mind to have you hanged too."

"Sire, I did but my duty; a soldier has but his orders. I didn't expect, after forty-seven years of faithful service, that my sovereign would think of putting me to a felon's death!"

"A hundred thousand plagues upon you! Can't you see that, while you are talking, my Bulbo is being hung!" screamed the princess.

"By Jove! she's always right, that girl, and I'm so absent," says the king, looking at his watch again. "Ha! there go the drums! What a doosid awkward thing, though!"

"O papa, you goose! Write the reprieve, and let me run with it," cries the princess, and she got a sheet of paper, and pen and ink, and laid them before the king.

"Confound it! Where are my spectacles?" the monarch exclaimed. "Angelica! Go up into my bed-room, look under my pillow—not your mamma's; there you'll see my keys. Bring them down to me, and—well, well! what impetuous things these girls are!" Angelica was

gone, and had run up panting to the bed-room, and found the keys,
and was back again before the king had finished a muffin. "Now,
love," says he, "you must go all the way back for my desk, in which
my spectacles are. If you *would* but have heard me out. . . . . Be
hanged to her! There she is off again! Angelica! ANGELICA!" When
his majesty called in his *loud* voice, she knew she must obey, and came
back.

"My dear, when you go out of a room, how often have I told you,
shut the door! That's a darling. That's all." At last the keys, and
the desk, and the spectacles were got, and the king mended his pen,
and signed his name to a reprieve, and Angelica ran with it as swift
as the wind. "You'd better stay, my love, and finish the muffins.
There's no use going. Be sure it's too late. Hand me over that raspberry jam, please," said the monarch. "Bong! Bawong! There goes
the half hour. I knew it was."

Angelica ran, and ran, and ran, and ran. She ran up Fore Street,
and down High Street, and through the market-place, and down to the
left, and over the bridge, and up the blind alley, and back again, and
round by the castle, and so along by the haberdasher's on the right,
opposite the lamp-post, and round the square, and she came—she
came to the *execution place*, where she saw Bulbo laying his head on
the block!!! The executioner raised his axe, but at that moment the
princess came panting up, and cried "Reprieve!" "Reprieve!"
screamed the princess. "Reprieve!" shouted all the people. Up the
scaffold stairs she sprang with the agility of a lighter of lamps, and
flinging herself in Bulbo's arms, regardless of all ceremony, she cried
out, "O my prince! my lord! my love! my Bulbo! Thine Angelica
has been in time to save thy precious existence, sweet rosebud; to
prevent thy being nipped in thy young bloom! Had aught befallen
thee, Angelica too had died, and welcomed death that joined her to
her Bulbo."

"H'm! there's no accounting for tastes," said Bulbo, looking so very

ANGELICA ARRIVES JUST IN TIME

much puzzled and uncomfortable, that the princess, in tones of tenderest strain, asked the cause of his disquiet.

"I tell you what it is, Angelica," said he, "since I came here yesterday, there has been such a row, and disturbance, and quarreling, and fighting, and chopping of heads off, and the deuce to pay, that I am inclined to go back to Crim Tartary."

"But with me as thy bride, my Bulbo! Though wherever thou art is Crim Tartary to me, my bold, my beautiful, my Bulbo!"

"Well, well, I suppose we must be married," says Bulbo. "Doctor, you came to read the Funeral Service—read the Marriage Service, will you? What must be, must. That will satisfy Angelica; and then, in the name of peace and quietness, do let us go back to breakfast."

Bulbo had carried a rose in his mouth all the time of the dismal ceremony. It was a fairy rose, and he was told by his mother that he ought never to part with it; so he had kept it between his teeth, even when he laid his poor head upon the block, hoping vaguely that some chance would turn up in his favor. As he began to speak to Angelica, he forgot about the rose, and of course it dropped out of his mouth. The romantic princess instantly stooped and seized it. "Sweet rose!" she exclaimed, "that bloomed upon my Bulbo's lip, never, never will I part from thee!" and she placed it in her bosom. And you know Bulbo *couldn't* ask her to give the rose back again. And they went to breakfast; and as they walked, it appeared to Bulbo that Angelica became more exquisitely lovely every moment.

He was frantic until they were married; and now, strange to say, it was Angelica who didn't care about him! He knelt down; he kissed her hand; he prayed and begged; he cried with admiration; while she, for her part, said she really thought they might wait; it seemed to her he was not handsome any more—no, not at all; quite the reverse; and not clever—no, very stupid; and not well bred, like Giglio —no, on the contrary, dreadfully vul—"

F

What, I can not say, for King Valoroso roared out, " *Pooh!* stuff!" in a terrible voice. " We will have no more of this shilly-shallying! Call the archbishop, and let the prince and princess be married off-hand!"

So married they were, and I am sure for my part, I trust they will be happy.

XII.

HOW BETSINDA FLED, AND WHAT BECAME OF HER.

BETSINDA wandered on and on, till she passed through the town gates, and so on the great Crim Tartary road, the very way on which Giglio too was going. "Ah!" thought she, as the diligence passed her, of which the conductor was blowing a delightful tune on his horn, "how I should like to be on that coach!" But the coach and the jingling horses were very soon gone. She little knew who was in it, though very likely she was thinking of him all the time.

Then came an empty cart, returning from market; and the driver, being a kind man, and seeing such a very pretty girl trudging along the road with bare feet, most good-naturedly gave her a seat. He said he lived on the confines of the forest, where his old father was a woodman, and, if she liked, he would take her so far on her road. All roads were the same to little Betsinda, so she very thankfully took this one.

And the carter put a cloth round her bare feet, and gave her some bread and cold bacon, and was very kind to her. For all that, she was very cold and melancholy. When after traveling on and on, evening came, and all the black pines were bending with snow, and there, at last, was the comfortable light beaming in the woodman's windows; and so they arrived, and went into his cottage. He was

an old man, and had a number of children, who were just at supper,
with nice hot bread and milk, when their elder brother arrived with
the cart.   And they jumped and clapped their hands ; for they were
good children, and he had brought them toys from the town.   And
when they saw the pretty stranger, they ran to her, and brought her
to the fire, and rubbed her poor little feet, and brought her bread and
milk.

" Look, father !" they said to the old woodman, " look at this poor
girl, and see what pretty cold feet she has.   They are as white as our
milk !   And look and see what an odd cloak she has, just like the bit
of velvet that hangs up in our cupboard, and which you found that
day the little cubs were killed by King Padella, in the forest !   And

look! why, bless us all! she has got round her neck just such another little shoe as that you brought home, and have shown us so often—a little blue velvet shoe!"

"What," said the old woodman, "what is all this about a shoe and a cloak ?"

And Betsinda explained that she had been left, when quite a little child, at the town with this cloak and this shoe. And the persons who had taken care of her had—had been angry with her for no fault, she hoped, of her own. And they had sent her away with her old clothes—and here, in fact, she was. She remembered having been in a forest, and—perhaps it was a dream—it was so very odd and strange--having lived in a cave with lions there ; and, before that, having lived in a very, very fine house, as fine as the king's, in the town.

When the woodman heard this, he was so astonished, it was quite curious to see how astonished he was. He went to his cupboard, and took out of a stocking a five-shilling piece of King Cavolfiore, and vowed it was exactly like the young woman. And then he produced

the shoe and piece of velvet which he had kept so long, and compared them with the things which Betsinda wore. In Betsinda's little shoe was written, "Hopkins, maker to the royal family ;" so in the other shoe was written, "Hopkins, maker to the royal family." In the in-

side of Betsinda's piece of cloak was embroidered, " PRIN ROSAL ;" in
the other piece of cloak was embroidered, " CESS BA.   No. 246 ;" so
that, when put together, you read, " PRINCESS ROSALBA.   No. 246."

On seeing this, the dear old woodman fell down on his knee, saying,
" O my princess, O my gracious royal lady, O my rightful Queen of
Crim Tartary ! I hail thee—I acknowledge thee—I do thee homage !"
And, in token of his fealty, he rubbed his venerable nose three times
on the ground, and put the princess's foot on his head.

" Why," said she, " my good woodman, you must be a nobleman
of my royal father's court !" for in her lowly retreat, and under the
name of Betsinda, HER MAJESTY, ROSALBA, Queen of Crim Tartary,
had read of the customs of all foreign courts and nations.

" Marry indeed am I, my gracious liege — the poor Lord Spinachi
once — the humble woodman these fifteen years syne, ever since the
tyrant Padella (may ruin overtake the treacherous knave !) dismissed
me from my post of first lord."

" First Lord of the Toothpick and Joint Keeper of the Snuff-box ?
I mind me !   Thou heldest these posts under our royal sire.   They are
restored to thee, Lord Spinachi !   I make thee knight of the second
class of our Order of the Pumpkin (the first class being reserved for
crowned heads alone).   Rise, Marquis of Spinachi !"   And, with indescribable majesty, the queen, who had no sword handy, waved the
pewter spoon with which she had been taking her bread and milk
over the bald head of the old nobleman, whose tears absolutely made
a puddle on the ground, and whose dear children went to bed that
night Lords and Ladies Bartolomeo, Ubaldo, Catarina, and Ottavia degli
Spinachi !

The acquaintance HER MAJESTY showed with the history and *noble
families* of her empire was wonderful.   " The house of Broccoli should
remain faithful to us," she said ; " they were ever welcome at our
court.   Have the Articiocchi, as was their wont, turned to the Rising
Sun ?   The family of Sauerkraut must sure be with us—they were

ever welcome in the halls of King Cavolfiore." And so she went on enumerating quite a list of the nobility and gentry of Crim Tartary, so admirably had her majesty profited by her studies while in exile.

The old Marquis of Spinachi said he could answer for them all; that the whole country groaned under Padella's tyranny, and longed to return to its rightful sovereign; and late as it was, he sent his children, who knew the forest well, to summon this nobleman and that; and when his eldest son, who had been rubbing the horse down and giving him his supper, came into the house for his own, the marquis told him to put his boots on, and a saddle on the mare, and ride hither and thither to such and such people.

When the young man heard who his companion in the cart had been, he too knelt down, and put her royal foot on his head; he too bedewed the ground with his tears; he was frantically in love with her, as every body now was who saw her; so were the young Lords Bartolomeo and Ubaldo, who punched each other's little heads out of jealousy; and so, when they came from east and west, at the summons of the Marquis degli Spinachi, were the Crim Tartar lords who still remained faithful to the house of Cavolfiore. They were such very old gentlemen, for the most part, that her majesty never suspected their absurd passion, and went among them quite unaware of the havoc her beauty was causing, until an old blind lord, who had joined her party, told her what the truth was; after which, for fear of making the people too much in love with her, she always wore a veil. She went about privately from one nobleman's castle to another, and they visited among themselves again, and had meetings, and composed proclamations and counter-proclamations, and distributed all the best places of the kingdom among one another, and selected who of the opposition party should be executed when the queen came to her own. And so, in about a year, they were ready to move.

The party of Fidelity was, in truth, composed of very feeble old fogies, for the most part; they went about the country waving their

old swords and flags, and calling " God save the queen !" and King
Padella happening to be absent upon an invasion, they had their own

way for a little; and to be sure the people were very enthusiastic
whenever they saw the queen.   Otherwise, the vulgar took matters
very quietly; for they said, as far as they could recollect, they were
pretty well as much taxed in Cavolfiore's time as now in Padella's

XIII.

HOW QUEEN ROSALBA CAME TO THE CASTLE OF THE BOLD COUNT HOGGINARMO.

HER MAJESTY, having indeed nothing else to give, made all her followers Knights of the Pumpkin, and marquises, earls, and baronets, and they had a little court for her, and made her a little crown of gilt paper, and a robe of cotton velvet; and they quarreled about the places to be given away in her court, and about rank, and precedence, and dignities—you can't think how they quarreled! The poor queen was very tired of her honors before she had them a month, and I dare say sighed sometimes even to be a lady's maid again. But we must all do our duty in our respective stations, so the queen resigned herself to perform hers.

We have said how it happened that none of the usurper's troops came out to oppose this Army of Fidelity: it pottered along as nimbly as the gout of the principal commanders allowed; it consisted of twice as many officers as soldiers, and at length passed near the estates of one of the most powerful noblemen of the country, who had not declared for the queen, but of whom her party had hopes, as he was always quarreling with King Padella.

When they came close to his park gates, this nobleman sent to say he would wait upon her majesty. He was a most powerful warrior, and his name was Count Hogginarmo, whose helmet it took two strong negroes to carry. He knelt down before her and said, " Madame and

liege lady! it becomes the great nobles of the Crimean realm to show every outward sign of respect to the wearer of the crown, whoever that may be. We testify to our own nobility in acknowledging yours. The bold Hogginarmo bends the knee to the first of the aristocracy of his country."

Rosalba said, "The bold Count of Hogginarmo was uncommonly kind." But she felt afraid of him, even while he was kneeling, and his eyes scowled at her from between his whiskers, which grew up to them.

"The first count of the empire, madam," he went on, "salutes the sovereign! The prince addresses himself to the not more noble lady! Madam, my hand is free, and I offer it, and my heart and my sword, to your service! My three wives lie buried in my ancestral vaults. The third perished but a year since; and this heart pines for a consort! Deign to be mine, and I swear to bring to your bridal table the head of King Padella, the eyes and nose of his son, Prince Bulbo, the right hand and ears of the usurping sovereign of Paflagonia, which country shall thenceforth be an appanage to your—to *our* crown! Say yes; Hogginarmo is not accustomed to be denied. Indeed, I can not contemplate the possibility of a refusal, for frightful will be the result; dreadful the murders; furious the devastations; horrible the tyranny; tremendous the tortures, misery, taxation, which the people of this realm will endure, if Hogginarmo's wrath be aroused! I see consent in your majesty's lovely eyes—their glances fill my soul with rapture!"

"O sir," Rosalba said, withdrawing her hand in great fright, "your lordship is exceedingly kind, but I am sorry to tell you that I have a prior attachment to a young gentleman of the name of—Prince—Giglio —and never—never can marry any one but him."

Who can describe Hogginarmo's wrath at this remark? Rising up from the ground, he ground his teeth so that fire flashed out of his mouth, from which, at the same time, issued remarks and language so *loud, violent, and improper*, that this pen shall never repeat them! "R-r-r-r-r—rejected! Fiends and perdition! The bold Hogginarmo rejected! All the world shall hear of my rage : and you, madam, you, above all, shall rue it!" And, kicking the two negroes before him, he rushed away, his whiskers streaming in the wind.

Her majesty's privy council was in a dreadful panic when they saw Hogginarmo issue from the royal presence in such a towering rage, making footballs of the poor negroes—a panic which the events justified. They marched off from Hogginarmo's park very crestfallen ; and in another half hour they were met by that rapacious chieftain with a few of his followers, who cut, slashed, charged, whacked, banged, and pommeled among them, took the queen prisoner, and drove the Army of Fidelity to I don't know where.

Poor queen! Hogginarmo, her conqueror, would not condescend to see her. "Get a horse-van!" he said to his grooms; "clap the hussy into it, and send her, with my compliments, to his majesty, King Padella."

Along with his lovely prisoner, Hogginarmo sent a letter full of servile compliments and loathsome flatteries to King Padella, for whose life and that of his royal family the *hypocritical humbug* pretended to offer the most fulsome prayers. And Hogginarmo promised speedily to pay his humble homage at his august master's throne, of which he begged leave to be counted the most loyal and constant defender. Such a *wary* old *bird* as King Padella was not to be caught by Master Hogginarmo's *chaff*, and we shall hear presently how the tyrant treated his upstart vassal. No, no; depend on't, two such rogues do not trust one another.

So this poor queen was laid in the straw like Margery Daw, and driven along in the dark ever so many miles to the court, where King Padella had now arrived, having vanquished all his enemies, murdered most of them, and brought some of the richest into captivity with him, for the purpose of torturing them and finding out where they had hidden their money.

Rosalba heard their shrieks and groans in the dungeon in which she was thrust—a most awful black hole, full of bats, rats, mice, toads, frogs, mosquitoes, bugs, fleas, serpents, and every kind of horror. No light was let into it, otherwise the jailers might have seen her and fallen in love with her, as an owl that lived up in the roof of the tower did; and a cat, you know, who can see in the dark, and, having set its green eyes on Rosalba, never would be got to go back to the turnkey's wife, to whom it belonged. And the toads in the dungeon came and kissed her feet, and the vipers wound round her neck and arms, and never hurt her, so charming was this poor princess in the midst of her misfortunes.

At last, after she had been kept in this place *ever so long*, the door of the dungeon opened, and the terrible KING PADELLA came in.

But what he said and did must be reserved for another chapter, as we must now go back to Prince Giglio.

XIV.

WHAT BECAME OF GIGLIO.

THE idea of marrying such an old creature as Gruffanuff frightened Prince Giglio so, that he ran up to his room, packed his trunks, fetched in a couple of porters, and was off to the diligence office in a twinkling.

It was well that he was so quick in his operations, did not dawdle over his luggage, and took the early coach ; for, as soon as the mistake about Prince Bulbo was found out, that cruel Glumboso sent up a couple of policemen to Prince Giglio's room, with orders that he should be carried to Newgate, and his head taken off before twelve o'clock. But the coach was out of the Paflagonian dominions before two o'clock ; and I dare say the express that was sent after Prince Giglio did not ride very quick, for many people in Paflagonia had a regard for Giglio, as the son of their old sovereign ; a prince, who, with all his weaknesses, was very much better than his brother the reigning, usurping, lazy, careless, passionate, tyrannical, reigning monarch. That prince busied himself with the balls, fêtes, masquerades, hunting parties, and so forth, which he thought proper to give on occasion of his daughter's marriage to Prince Bulbo ; and, let us trust, was not sorry in his own heart that his brother's son had escaped the scaffold.

It was very cold weather, and the snow was on the ground, and Giglio, who gave his name as simple Mr. Gills, was very glad to get a comfortable place in the coupé of the diligence, where he sat with the conductor and another gentleman.   At the first stage from Blombodinga, as they stopped to change horses, there came up to the dili-

gence a very ordinary, vulgar-looking woman, with a bag under her arm, who asked for a place.   All the inside places were taken, and

the young woman was informed that if she wished to travel, she
must go upon the roof; and the passenger inside with Giglio (a rude
person, I should think) put his head out of the window, and said,
" Nice weather for traveling outside! I wish you a pleasant journey,

my dear."   The poor woman coughed very much, and Giglio pitied
her.   " I will give up my place to her," says he, " rather than she
should travel in the cold air with that horrid cough."   On which the
vulgar traveler said, " You'd keep her warm, I am sure, if it's a *muff*
she wants."   On which Giglio pulled his nose, boxed his ears, hit him
in the eye, and gave this vulgar person a warning never to call him
muff again.

Then he sprang up gayly on to the roof of the diligence, and made
himself very comfortable in the straw. The vulgar traveler got
down only at the next station, and Giglio took his place again, and
talked to the person next to him. She appeared to be a most agreeable, well-informed, and entertaining female. They traveled to-

G

gether till night, and she gave Giglio all sorts of things out of the
bag which she carried, and which, indeed, seemed to contain the
most wonderful collection of articles. He was thirsty — out there
came a pint bottle of Bass's pale ale, and a silver mug! Hungry—
she took out a cold fowl, some slices of ham, bread, salt, and a most
delicious piece of cold plum-pudding, and a little glass of brandy afterward.

As they traveled, this plain-looking, queer woman talked to Giglio
on a variety of subjects, in which the poor prince showed his ignorance as much as she did her capacity. He owned, with many
blushes, how ignorant he was; on which the lady said, "My dear
Giigl—my good Mr. Gills, you are a young man, and have plenty of
time before you. You have nothing to do but to improve yourself.
Who knows but that you may find use for your knowledge some
day, when — when you may be wanted at home, as some people
may be?"

"Good heavens, madam!" says he, "do you know me?"

"I know a number of funny things," says the lady. "I have
been at some people's christenings, and turned away from other
folk's doors. I have seen some people spoiled by good fortune,
and others, as I hope, improved by hardship. I advise you to stay
at the town where the coach stops for the night. Stay there
and study, and remember your old friend to whom you were
kind."

"And who is my old friend?" asked Giglio.

"When you want any thing," says the lady, "look in this bag, which
I leave to you as a present, and be grateful to—"

"To whom, madam?" says he.

"To the Fairy Blackstick," says the lady, flying out of the window. And when Giglio asked the conductor if he knew where the
lady was,

"What lady?" says the man. "There has been no lady in this

coach, except the old woman, who got out at the last stage." And
Giglio thought he had been dreaming. But there was the bag which
Blackstick had given him lying on his lap; and when he came to the
town, he took it in his hand, and went into the inn.

They gave him a very bad bed-room; and Giglio, when he woke in
the morning, fancying himself in the royal palace at home, called,
"John! Charles! Thomas! My chocolate! my dressing-gown! my
slippers!" But nobody came. There was no bell, so he went and
bawled out for waiter on the top of the stairs.

The landlady came up, looking—looking like this—

"What are you a hollaring and a bellaring for here, young man'"
says she.

"There's no warm water—no servants; my boots are not even
cleaned."

"He, he! Clean 'em yourself," says the landlady. "You young
students give yourselves pretty airs. I never heard such impudence."

"I'll quit the house this instant," says Giglio.

"The sooner the better, young man. Pay your bill and be off. All
my rooms is wanted for gentlefolks, and not for such as you."

"You may well keep the Bear Inn," said Giglio. "You should
have yourself painted as the sign."

The landlady of the Bear went away *growling*. And Giglio returned to his room, where the first thing he saw was the fairy bag lying
on the table, which seemed to give a little hop as he came in. "I
hope it has some breakfast in it," says Giglio, "for I have only a very
little money left." But on opening the bag, what do you think was

there? A blacking-brush and a pot of Warren's jet, and on the pot
was written,

> " Poor young men their boots must black.
> Use me, and cork me, and put me back."

So Giglio laughed and blacked his boots, and put back the brush and the bottle into the bag.

When he had done dressing himself, the bag gave another little hop, and he went to it and took out—

    1. A table-cloth and a napkin.

    2. A sugar-basin full of the best loaf sugar.

    4, 6, 8, 10. Two forks, two teaspoons, two knives, and a pair of sugar-tongs, and a butter-knife, all marked G.

    11, 12, 13. A tea-cup, saucer, and slop-basin.

    14. A jug full of delicious cream.

    15. A canister with black tea and green.

    16. A large tea-urn and boiling water.

    17. A saucepan, containing three eggs nicely done.

    18. A quarter of a pound of best Epping butter.

    19. A brown loaf.

And if he hadn't enough now for a good breakfast, I should like to know who ever had one.

Giglio, having had his breakfast, popped all the things back into the bag, and went out looking for lodgings. I forgot to say that this celebrated university town was called Bosforo.

He took a modest lodging opposite the schools, paid his bill at the inn, and went to his apartment with his trunk, carpet bag, and not forgetting, we may be sure, his *other* bag.

When he opened his trunk, which the day before he had filled with his best clothes, he found it contained only books. And in the first of them which he opened there was written,

> " Clothes for the back, books for the head :
> Read, and remember them when they are read."

And in his bag, when Giglio looked in it, he found a student's cap and gown, a writing-book full of paper, an inkstand, pens, and a Johnson's Dictionary, which was very useful to him, as his spelling had been sadly neglected.

So he sat down, and worked away very, very hard for a whole year, during which "Mr. Giles" was quite an example to all the students in the University of Bosforo. He never got into any riots or disturbances. The professors all spoke well of him, and the students liked him too; so that when, at examination, he took all the prizes, viz.,

The Spelling Prize,	The French Prize,
The Writing Prize,	The Arithmetic Prize,
The History Prize,	The Latin Prize,
The Catechism Prize,	The Good Conduct Prize,

all his fellow-students said, "Hurray! Hurray for Giles! Giles is the boy—the students' joy! Hurray for Giles!" And he brought quite a quantity of medals, crowns, books, and tokens of distinction home to his lodgings.

One day after the examinations, as he was diverting himself at a coffee-house with two friends (did I tell you that in his bag, every Saturday night, he found just enough to pay his bills, with a guinea over, for pocket-money? Didn't I tell you? Well, he did, as sure as twice twenty makes forty-five), he chanced to look in the "Bosforo Chronicle," and read off, quite easily (for he could spell, read, and write the longest words now), the following:

" ROMANTIC CIRCUMSTANCE.—One of the most extraordinary adventures that we have ever heard has set the neighboring country of Crim Tartary in a state of great excitement.

" It will be remembered that when the present revered sovereign of Crim Tartery, his majesty, King *Padella*, took possession of the throne, after having vanquished, in the terrific battle of Blunderbusco, the late King *Cavolfiore*, that prince's only child, the Princess Rosalba,

was not found in the royal palace, of which King Padella took possession, and, it was said, had strayed into the forest (being abandoned by
all her attendants), where she had been eaten up by those ferocious
lions, the last pair of which were captured some time since, and brought
to the Tower, after killing several hundred persons.

"His majesty, King Padella, who has the kindest heart in the world,
was grieved at the accident which had occurred to the harmless little princess, for whom his majesty's known benevolence would certainly have provided a fitting establishment. But her death seemed
to be certain. The mangled remains of a cloak, and a little shoe,
were found in the forest during a hunting party, in which the intrepid sovereign of Crim Tartary slew two of the lions' cubs with his
own spear. And these interesting relics of an innocent little creature were carried home and kept by their finder, the Baron Spinachi,
formerly an officer in Cavolfiore's household. The baron was dis-
graced in consequence of his known legitimist opinions, and has lived
for some time in the humble capacity of a wood-cutter, in a forest on
the outskirts of the kingdom of Crim Tartary.

"Last Tuesday week, Baron Spinachi, and a number of gentlemen
attached to the former dynasty, appeared in arms, crying 'God save
Rosalba, the first queen of Crim Tartary!' and surrounding a lady
whom report describes as '*beautiful exceedingly*.' Her history *may* be
authentic, *is* certainly most romantic.

"The personage calling herself Rosalba states that she was brought
out of the forest fifteen years since by a lady in a car drawn by
dragons (this account is certainly *improbable*); that she was left in
the palace garden of Blombodinga, where her Royal Highness the
Princess Angelica, now married to his Royal Highness Bulbo, Crown
Prince of Crim Tartary, found the child, and, with *that elegant benevolence* which has always distinguished the heiress of the throne
of Paflagonia, gave the little outcast a *shelter and a home!* Her
parentage not being known, and her garb very humble, the found-

ling was educated in the palace in a menial capacity, under the name
of *Betsinda*.

"She did not give satisfaction, and was dismissed, carrying with
her, certainly, part of a mantle and a shoe which she had on when
first found. According to her statement, she quitted Blombodinga
about a year ago, since which time she has been with the Spinachi
family. On the very same morning, the Prince Giglio, nephew to the
King of Paflagonia, a young prince whose character for *talent* and
order were, to say truth, *none of the highest*, also quitted Blombodinga,
and has not been since heard of!"

"What an extraordinary story!" said Smith and Jones, two young
students, Giglio's especial friends.

"Ha! what is this?" Giglio went on, reading—

"SECOND EDITION, EXPRESS.—We hear that the troop under Baron
Spinachi has been surrounded, and utterly routed, by General Count
Hogginarmo, and the *soi-disant* princess is sent a prisoner to the
capital.

"UNIVERSITY NEWS.—Yesterday, at the schools, the distinguished
young student, Mr. Giles, read a Latin oration, and was complimented
by the Chancellor of Bosforo, Dr. Pruguaro, with the highest University honor—the wooden spoon."

"Never mind that stuff," says *Giles*, greatly disturbed. "Come
home with me, my friends. Gallant Smith! intrepid Jones! friends
of my studies—partakers of my academic toils—I have that to tell
shall astonish your honest minds."

"Go it, old boy!" cried the impetuous Smith.

"Talk away, my buck!" says Jones, a lively fellow.

With an air of indescribable dignity, Giglio checked their natural,
but no more seemly familiarity. "Jones, Smith, my good friends,"
said the PRINCE, "disguise is henceforth useless; I am no more the
humble student Giles—I am the descendant of a royal line."

"*Atavis edite regibus.* I know, old co——," cried Jones—he was

TO ARMS!

going to say old cock, but a flash from THE ROYAL EYE again awed him.

"Friends," continued the prince, "I am that Giglio—I am, in fact, Paflagonia. Rise, Smith, and kneel not in the public street. Jones, thou true heart! My faithless uncle, when I was a baby, filched from me that brave crown my father left me, bred me all young and careless of my rights, like unto hapless Hamlet, Prince of Denmark; and had I any thoughts about my wrongs, soothed me with promises of near redress. I should espouse his daughter, young Angelica; we two, indeed, should reign in Paflagonia. His words were false—false as Angelica's heart! false as Angelica's hair, color, front teeth! She looked with her skew eyes upon young Bulbo, Crim Tartary's stupid heir, and she preferred him. 'Twas then I turned my eyes upon Betsinda—Rosalba, as she now is. And I saw in her the blushing sum of all perfection—the pink of maiden modesty—the nymph that my fond heart had ever woo'd in dreams," &c., &c.

(I don't give this speech, which was very fine, but very long; and though Smith and Jones knew nothing about the circumstances, my dear reader does, so I go on.)

The prince and his young friends hastened home to his apartments, highly excited by the intelligence, as no doubt by the *royal narrator's* admirable manner of recounting it, and they ran up to his room where he had worked so hard at his books.

On his writing-table was his bag, grown so long that the prince could not help remarking it. He went to it, opened it, and what do you think he found in it?

A splendid long, gold-handled, red-velvet-scabbarded cut-and-thrust sword, and on the sheath was embroidered "ROSALBA FOREVER!"

He drew out the sword, which flashed and illuminated the whole room, and called out "Rosalba forever!" Smith and Jones following him, but quite respectfully this time, and taking the time from his royal highness.

And now his trunk opened with a sudden pong, and out there came three ostrich feathers in a gold crown, surrounding a beautiful shining steel helmet, a cuirass, a pair of spurs, finally a complete suit of armor.

The books on Giglio's shelves were all gone. Where there had been some great dictionaries, Giglio's friends found two pairs of jack-boots, labeled "Lieutenant Smith," "— Jones, Esq.," which fitted them to a nicety. Besides, there were helmets, back and breast plates, swords, &c., just like in Mr. G. P. R. James's novels, and that evening three cavaliers might have been seen issuing from the gates of Bosforo, in whom the porters, proctors, &c., never thought of recognizing the young prince and his friends.

They got horses at a livery-stable-keeper's, and never drew bridle until they reached the last town on the frontier before you come to Crim Tartary. Here, as their animals were tired, and the cavaliers hungry, they stopped and refreshed at an hostel. I could make a chapter of this if I were like some writers, but I like to cram my measure tight down, you see, and give you a great deal for your money, and, in a word, they had some bread, and cheese, and ale up stairs on the balcony of the inn. As they were drinking, drums and trumpets sounded nearer and nearer, the market-place was filled with soldiers, and his royal highness, looking forth, recognized the Paflagonian banners, and the Paflagonian national air which the bands were playing.

The troops all made for the tavern at once, and as they came up, Giglio exclaimed, on beholding their leader, " Whom do I see? Yes! No! It is, it is! Phoo! No, it can't be! Yes! it is my friend, my gallant faithful veteran, Captain Hedzoff! Ho! Hedzoff! Knowest thou not thy prince—thy Giglio? Good corporal, methinks we once were friends. Ha! sergeant, an my memory serves me right, we have had many a bout at single-stick."

" I'faith, we have a many, good my lord," says the sergeant.

PRINCE GIGLIO'S SPEECH TO THE ARMY

" Tell me, what means this mighty armament," continued his royal highness from the balcony, " and whither march my Paflagonians ?"

Hedzoff's head fell. " My lord," he said, " we march as the allies of great Padella, Crim Tartary's monarch."

" Crim Tartary's usurper, gallant Hedzoff! Crim Tartary's grim tyrant, honest Hedzoff!" said the prince, on the balcony, quite sarcastically.

" A soldier, prince, must needs obey his orders : mine are to help his majesty, Padella. And also (though alack that I should say it') to seize, wherever I should light upon him—"

" First catch your hare! ha, Hedzoff?" exclaimed his royal highness.

" —On the body of *Giglio*, whilome Prince of Paflagonia." Hedzoff went on, with indescribable emotion. " My prince, give up your sword without ado. Look ! we are thirty thousand men to one !"

" Give up my sword ! Giglio give up his sword !" cried the prince ; and, stepping well forward on to the balcony, the royal youth, *without preparation*, delivered a speech so magnificent that no report can do justice to it. It was all in blank verse (in which, from this time, he invariably spoke, as more becoming his majestic station.) It lasted for three days and three nights, during which not a single person who heard him was tired, or remarked the difference between daylight and dark, the soldiers only cheering tremendously, when occasionally, once in nine hours, the prince paused to suck an orange, which Jones took out of the bag. He explained, in terms which we say we shall not attempt to convey, the whole history of the previous transaction, and his determination not only not to give up his sword, but to assume his rightful crown. And at the end of this extraordinary, this truly *gigantic* effort, Captain Hedzoff flung up his helmet, and cried, " Hurray ! Hurray ! Long live King Giglio !"

Such were the consequences of having employed his time well at college!

When the excitement had ceased, beer was ordered out for the army, and their sovereign himself did not disdain a little! And now it was with some alarm that Captain Hedzoff told him his division was only the advanced guard of the Paflagonian contingent hastening to King Padella's aid, the main force being a day's march in the rear, under His Royal Highness Prince Bulbo.

"We will wait here, good friend, to beat the prince," his majesty said, "and *then* will make his royal father wince."

XV.

WE RETURN TO ROSALBA.

KING PADELLA made very similar proposals to Rosalba to those which she had received from the various princes who, as we have seen, had fallen in love with her. His majesty was a widower, and offered to marry his fair captive that instant; but she declined his invitation in her usual polite manner, stating that Prince Giglio was her love, and that any other union was out of the question. Having tried tears and supplications in vain, this violent-tempered monarch menaced her with threats and tortures; but she declared she would rather suffer all these than accept the hand of her father's murderer, who left her finally, uttering the most awful imprecations, and bidding her prepare for death the following morning.

All night long the king spent in advising how he should get rid of this obdurate young creature. Cutting off her h ad was much too easy a death for her; hanging was so common in his majesty's dominions, that it no longer afforded him any sport; finally, he bethought himself of a pair of fierce lions which had lately been sent to him as presents, and he determined, with these ferocious brutes, to hunt poor Rosalba down. Adjoining his castle was an amphitheatre, where the prince indulged in bull-baiting, rat-hunting, and oth r ferocious sports. The two lions were kept in a cage under this place; their roaring might be heard over the whole city, the inhabitants of which, I am sorry to say, thronged in numbers to see a poor young lady gobbled up by two wild beasts.

The king took his place in the royal box, having the officers of his court around, and the Count Hogginarmo by his side, upon whom his majesty was observed to look very fiercely; the fact is, royal spies had

II

told the monarch of Hogginarmo's behavior, his proposals to Rosalba, and his offer to fight for the crown. Black as thunder looked King Padella at this proud noble, as they sat in the front seats of the theatre, waiting to see the tragedy whereof poor Rosalba was to be the heroine.

At length that princess was brought out in her night-gown, with all her beautiful hair falling down her back, and looking so pretty, that even the beef-eaters and keepers of the wild animals wept plentifully at seeing her. And she walked with her poor little feet (only, luckily, the arena was covered with sawdust), and went and leaned up against a great stone in the centre of the amphitheatre, round which the court and the people were seated in boxes with bars before them, for fear of the great, fierce, red-maned, black-throated, long-tailed, roaring, bellowing, rushing lions. And now the gates were opened, and, with a wurrawarrurawarar, two great lean, hungry, roaring lions rushed out

of their den, where they had been kept for three weeks on nothing but a little toast and water, and dashed straight up to the stone where poor Rosalba was waiting. Commend her to your patron saints, all you kind people, for she is in a dreadful state!

There was a hum and a buzz all through the circus, and the fierce King Padella even felt a little compassion. But Count Hogginarmo, seated by his majesty, roared out, "Hurray! Now for it! Soo-soo-soo!"

that nobleman being uncommonly angry still at Rosalba's refusal of
him.

But, O strange event! O remarkable circumstance! O extraordinary coincidence, which I am sure none of you could, *by any possibility*,
have divined! When the lions came to Rosalba, instead of devouring
her with their great teeth, it was with kisses they gobbled her up!
They licked her pretty feet, they nuzzled their noses in her lap, they
moo'd, they seemed to say, "Dear, dear sister, don't you recollect your
brothers in the forest?" And she put her pretty white arms round
their tawny necks, and kissed them.

King Padella was immensely astonished. The Count Hogginarmo
was extremely disgusted. "Pooh!" the count cried. "Gammon!"
exclaimed his lordship. "These lions are tame beasts come from
Wombwell's or Astley's. It is a shame to put people off in this way.
I believe they are little boys dressed up in door-mats. They are no
lions at all."

Ha!" said the king; "you dare to say 'gammon' to your sovereign,
do you? These lions are no lions at all, arn't they? Ho! my beef-
eaters! Ho! my body-guard! Take this Count Hogginarmo, and fling
him into the circus! Give him a sword and buckler; let him keep
his armor on, and his weather-eye out, and fight these lions."

The haughty Hogginarmo laid down his opera-glass, and looked
scowling round at the king and his attendants. "Touch me not,
dogs!" he said, "or, by St. Nicholas the elder, I will gore you! Your
majesty thinks Hogginarmo is afraid? No, not of a hundred thousand
lions! Follow me down into the circus, King Padella, and match thyself against one of you brutes. Thou darest not. Let them both come
on, then!" And, opening a grating of the box, he jumped lightly down
into the circus.

Wurra wurra wurra wur-aw-aw-aw!!!
In about two minutes
the Count Hogginarmo was
GOBBLED UP
by
those lions,
bones, boots, and all,
and
there was an
end of him.

At this, the king said, "Serve him right, the rebellious ruffian!
And now, as those lions won't eat that young woman—"

"Let her off! let her off!" cried the crowd.

"NO!" roared the king. "Let the beef-eaters go down and chop
her into small pieces. If the lions defend her, let the archers shoot
them to death. That hussy shall die in tortures!"

"A-a-ah!" cried the crowd. "Shame! shame!"

"Who dares cry out shame?" cried the furious potentate (so little
can tyrants command their passions). "Fling any scoundrel who says
a word down among the lions!" I warrant you there was a dead silence then, which was broken by a pang arang pang pangkarangpang,
and a knight and a herald rode in at the farther end of the circus—
the knight in full armor, with his vizor up, and bearing a letter on
the point of his lance.

"Ha!" exclaimed the king; "by my fay, 'tis Elephant and Castle,
pursuivant of my brother of Paflagonia; and the knight, as my memory serves me, is the gallant Captain Hedzoff. What news from Paflagonia, gallant Hedzoff? Elephant and Castle, beshrew me, thy
trumpeting must have made thee thirsty. What will my trusty herald like to drink?"

"Bespeaking first safe conduct from your lordship," said Captain

Hedzoff, " before we take a drink of any thing, permit us to deliver our king's message."

" My lordship, ha!" said Crim Tartary, frowning terrifically. " That title soundeth strange in the anointed ears of a crowned king. Straightway speak out your message, knight and herald!"

Reigning up his charger in a most elegant manner close under the king's balcony, Hedzoff turned to the herald, and bade him begin.

Elephant and Castle, dropping his trumpet over his shoulder, took a large sheet of paper out of his hat, and began to read:

" O Yes! O Yes! O Yes! Know all men by these presents, that we, Giglio, King of Paflagonia, Grand Duke of Cappadocia, Sovereign Prince of Turkey and the Sausage Islands, having assumed our rightful throne and title, long time falsely borne by our usurping uncle, styling himself King of Paflagonia—"

" Ha!" growled Padella.

" Hereby summon the false traitor, Padella, calling himself King of Crim Tartary—"

The king's curses were dreadful. " Go on, Elephant and Castle!" said the intrepid Hedzoff.

" To release from cowardly imprisonment his liege lady and rightful sovereign, Rosalba, Queen of Crim Tartary, and restore her to her royal throne: in default of which, I, Giglio, proclaim the said Padella sneak, traitor, humbug, usurper, and coward. I challenge him to meet me, with fists or with pistols, with battle-axe or sword, with blunderbuss or single-stick, alone or at the head of his army, on foot or on horseback, and will prove my words upon his wicked, ugly body!"

" God save the king!" said Captain Hedzoff, executing a demivolte, two semilunes, and three caracoles.

" Is that all?" said Padella, with the terrific calm of concentrated fury.

" That, sir, is all my royal master's message. Here is his majesty's letter in autograph, and here is his glove, and if any gentleman of

Crim Tartary chooses to find fault with his majesty's expressions, I, Tuffskin Hedzoff, captain of the guard, am very much at his service," and he waved his lance, and looked at the assembly all round.

"And what says my good brother of Paflagonia, my dear son's father-in-law to this rubbish?" asked the king.

"The king's uncle hath been deprived of the crown he unjustly wore," said Hedzoff, gravely. "He and his ex-minister, Glumboso, are now in prison, waiting the sentence of my royal master. After the battle of Bombardaro—"

"Of what?" asked the surprised Padella.

"Of Bombardaro, where my liege, his present majesty, would have performed prodigies of valor, but that the whole of his uncle's army came over to our side, with the exception of Prince Bulbo."

"Ah! my boy, my boy, my Bulbo was no traitor!" cried Padella.

"Prince Bulbo, far from coming over to us, ran away, sir; but I caught him. The prince is a prisoner in our army, and the most terrific tortures await him if a hair of the Princess Rosalba's head is injured."

"Do they?" exclaimed the furious Padella, who was now perfectly livid with rage. "Do they, indeed? So much the worse for Bulbo. I've twenty sons as lovely each as Bulbo. Not one but is as fit to reign as Bulbo. Whip, whack, flog, starve, rack, punish, torture Bulbo—break all his bones—roast him or flay him alive—pull all his pretty teeth out one by one! But, justly dear as Bulbo is to me—joy of my eyes, fond treasure of my soul!—ha, ha, ha, ha! revenge is dearer still. Ho! torturers, rack-men, executioners, light up the fires and make the pincers hot! Get lots of boiling lead! Bring out ROSALBA!"

XVI.

HOW HEDZOFF RODE BACK AGAIN TO KING GIGLIO.

CAPTAIN HEDZOFF rode away when King Padella uttered this cruel command, having done his duty in delivering the message with which his royal master had intrusted him. Of course he was very sorry for Rosalba, but what could he do?

So he returned to King Giglio's camp, and found the young monarch in a disturbed state of mind, smoking cigars in the royal tent. His majesty's agitation was not appeased by the news that was brought by his embassador. "The brutal, ruthless ruffian! royal wretch!" Giglio exclaimed. "As England's poesy has well remarked, 'The man that lays his hand upon a woman, save in the way of kindness, is a villain.' Ha, Hedzoff?"

"That he is, your majesty," said the attendant.

"And did'st thou see her flung into the oil? and didn't the soothing oil—the emollient oil, refuse to boil, good Hedzoff—and to spoil the fairest lady ever eyes did look on?"

"Faith, good my liege, I had no heart to look and see a beauteous lady boiling down; I took your royal message to Padella, and bore his back to you. I told him you would hold Prince Bulbo answerable. He only said that he had twenty sons as good as Bulbo, and forthwith he bade the ruthless executioners proceed."

"O cruel father—O unhappy son," cried the king. "Go, some of you, and bring Prince Bulbo hither."

Bulbo was brought in chains, looking very uncomfortable. Though a prisoner, he had been tolerably happy, perhaps because his mind was at rest, and all the fighting was over, and he was playing at marbles with his guards when the king sent for him.

"O my poor Bulbo," said his majesty, with looks of infinite compassion, "hast thou heard the news" (for you see Giglio wanted to break the thing gently to the prince)? "Thy brutal father has condemned Rosalba—p-p-p-put her to death, P-p-p-prince Bulbo!"

"What! killed Betsinda! boo-hoo-hoo!" cried out Bulbo; "Betsinda! pretty Betsinda! dear Betsinda! She was the dearest little girl in the world. I love her better twenty thousand times even than Angelica," and he went on expressing his grief in so hearty and unaffected a manner, that the king was quite touched by it, and said, shaking Bulbo's hand, that he wished he had known Bulbo sooner.

Bulbo, quite unconsciously, and meaning for the best, offered to come and sit with his majesty, and smoke a cigar with him, and console him. The *royal kindness* supplied Bulbo with a cigar; he had not had one, he said, since he was taken prisoner.

And now think what must have been the feelings of the most *merciful of monarchs*, when he informed his prisoner that, in consequence of King Padella's *cruel and dastardly behavior* to Rosalba, Prince Bulbo must instantly be executed! The noble Giglio could not restrain his tears, nor could the grenadiers, nor the officers, nor could Bulbo himself, when the matter was explained to him; and he was brought to understand that his majesty's promise, of course, was *above every thing*, and Bulbo must submit. So poor Bulbo was led out, Hedzoff trying to console him by pointing out that if he had won the battle of Bombardaro, he might have hanged Prince Giglio. "Yes! but that is no comfort to me now!" said poor Bulbo; nor indeed was it, poor fellow!

He was told the business would be done the next morning at eight, and was taken back to his dungeon, where every attention was paid to him. The jailer's wife sent him tea, and the turnkey's daughter begged him to write his name in her album, where a many gentlemen had wrote it on like occasions! "Bother your album!" says Bulbo. The undertaker came and measured him for the handsomest coffin which money could buy—even this didn't console Bulbo. The cook brought him dishes which he once used to like, but he wouldn't touch

them. He sat down and began writing an adieu to Angelica, as the clock kept always ticking, and the hands drawing nearer to next morning. The barber came in at night, and offered to shave him for the next day. Prince Bulbo kicked him away, and went on writing a few words to Princess Angelica, as the clock kept always ticking, and the hands hopping nearer and nearer to next morning. He got up on the

top of a hat-box, on the top of a chair, on the top of his bed, on the top
of his table, and looked out to see whether he might escape, as the

clock kept always ticking, and the hands drawing nearer, and nearer,
and nearer.

But looking out of the window was one thing, and jumping another:
and the town clock struck seven. So he got into bed for a little sleep,
but the jailer came and woke him, and said, "Git up, your royal igh-
ness, if you please; it's *ten minutes to eight!*"

So poor Bulbo got up: he had gone to bed in his clothes (the lazy
boy), and he shook himself, and said he didn't mind about dressing,
or having any breakfast, thank you; and he saw the soldiers who had

come for him.   "Lead on!" he said; and they led the way, deeply

affected; and they came into the court-yard, and out into the square,
and there was King Giglio come to take leave of him, and his majesty
most kindly shook hands with him, and the *gloomy procession* marched
on—when hark!

Haw—wurraw—wurraw—aworr!

A roar of wild beasts was heard.   And who should come riding into
the town, frightening away the boys, and even the beadle and police-
man, but ROSALBA!

The fact is, that when Captain Hedzoff entered into the court of
Snapdragon Castle, and was discoursing with King Padella, the lions

made a dash at the open gate, gobbled up the six beef-eaters in a jiffy, and away they went with Rosalba on the back of one of them, and they carried her, turn and turn about, till they came to the city where Prince Giglio's army was encamped.

When the KING heard of the QUEEN's arrival, you may think how he rushed out of his breakfast-room to hand her majesty off her lion! The lions were grown as fat as pigs now, having had Hogginarmo and all those beef-eaters, and were so tame any body might pat them.

While Giglio knelt (most gracefully) and helped the princess, Bulbo,

for his part, rushed up and kissed the lion. He flung his arms round
the forest monarch; he hugged him, and laughed and cried for joy.
" O you darling old beast, O how glad I am to see you, and the dear,
dear Bets"—that is, Rosalba.

" What, is it you? Poor Bulbo!" said the queen. " O how glad I am
to see you;" and she gave him her hand to kiss. King Giglio slapped
him most kindly on the back, and said, " Bulbo, my boy, I am delighted, for your sake, that her majesty has arrived."

" So am I," said Bulbo; " and *you know why.*" Captain Hedzoff
here came up. " Sire, it is half past eight: shall we proceed with
the execution?"

" Execution! what for?" asked Bulbo.

" An officer only knows his orders," replied Captain Hedzoff, show-
ing his warrant, on which his majesty King Giglio smilingly said,
" Prince Bulbo was reprieved this time," and most graciously invited
him to breakfast.

XVII.

HOW A TREMENDOUS BATTLE TOOK PLACE, AND WHO WON IT.

As soon as King Padella heard, what we know already, that his victim, the lovely Rosalba, had escaped him, his majesty's fury knew no bounds, and he pitched the lord chancellor, lord chamberlain, and every officer of the crown whom he could set eyes on, into the caldron of boiling oil prepared for the princess. Then he ordered his whole army, horse, foot, and artillery, and set forth at the head of an innumerable host, and I should think twenty thousand drummers, trumpeters, and fifers.

King Giglio's advanced guard, you may be sure, kept that monarch acquainted with the enemy's dealings, and he was in nowise disconcerted. He was much too polite to alarm the princess, his lovely guest, with any unnecessary rumors of battles impending; on the contrary, he did every thing to amuse and divert her, gave her a most elegant breakfast, dinner, lunch, and got up a ball for her that evening when he danced with her every single dance.

Poor Bulbo was taken into favor again, and allowed to go quite free now. He had new clothes given him, was called "my good cousin" by his majesty, and was treated with the greatest distinction by every body. But it was easy to see he was very melancholy. The fact is, the sight of Betsinda, who looked perfectly lovely in an elegant new dress, set poor Bulbo frantic in love with her again. And he never thought about Angelica, now Princess Bulbo, whom he had left at home, and who, as we know, did not care much about him.

The king, dancing the twenty-fifth polka with Rosalba, remarked with wonder the ring she wore ; and then Rosalba told him how she had got it from Gruffanuff, who, no doubt, had picked it up when Angelica flung it away.

" Yes," says the Fairy Blackstick, who had come to see the young people, and who had, very likely, certain plans regarding them, " that ring I gave the queen, Giglio's mother, who was not, saving your presence, a very wise woman ; it is enchanted, and whoever wears it looks beautiful in the eyes of the world   I made poor Prince Bulbo, when he was christened, the present of a rose, which made him look handsome while he had it ; but he gave it to Angelica, who instantly looked beautiful again, while Bulbo relapsed into his natural plainness."

" Rosalba needs no ring, I am sure," says Giglio, with a low bow. " She is beautiful enough, in my eyes, without any enchanted aid."

" O sir !" said Rosalba.

" Take off the ring and try." said the king : and he resolutely drew the ring off her finger.   In *his* eyes she looked just as handsome as before!

The king was thinking of throwing the ring away, as it was so dangerous, and made all the people so mad about Rosalba ; but, being a prince of great humor, and good humor too, he cast his eyes upon a poor youth who happened to be looking on very disconsolately, and said,

" Bulbo, my poor lad ! come and try on this ring.   The Princess Rosalba makes it a present to you."   The magic properties of this ring were uncommonly strong, for no sooner had Bulbo put it on, than, lo and behold ! he appeared a personable, agreeable young prince enough, with a fine complexion, fair hair, rather stout, and with bandy legs ; but these were encased in such a beautiful pair of yellow morocco boots, that nobody remarked them.   And Bulbo's spirits rose up almost immediately after he had looked in the glass, and he talked to their majesties in the most lively, agreeable manner, and danced opposite the queen with one of the prettiest maids of honor, and after looking at her majesty, could not help saying, " How very odd ; she is very pretty, but not so *extraordinarily* handsome." " Oh no, by no means!" says the maid of honor.

" But what care I, dear sir," says the queen, who overheard them, " if *you* think I am good-looking enough ?"

His majesty's glance in reply to this affectionate speech was such that no painter could draw it. And the Fairy Blackstick said, " Bless you, my darling children ! Now you are united and happy ; and now you see what I said from the first, that a little misfortune has done you both good. *You*, Giglio, had you been bred in prosperity, would scarcely have learned to read or write—you would have been idle and extravagant, and could not have been a good king, as now you will be. You, Rosalba, would have been so flattered, that your little head might have been turned like Angelica's, who thought herself too good for Giglio."

" As if any body could be good enough for *him*," cried Rosalba.

" Oh, you, you darling!" says Giglio. And so she was ; and he was just holding out his arms in order to give her a hug before the whole company, when a messenger came rushing in, and said, " My lord, the enemy!"

" To arms !" cries Giglio.

" Oh, mercy !" says Rosalba, and fainted, of course. He snatched one kiss from her lips, and rushed *forth to the field* of battle !

The fairy had provided King Giglio with a suit of armor, which was not only embroidered all over with jewels, and blinding to your eyes to look at, but was water-proof, gun-proof, and sword-proof ; so that in the midst of the very hottest battles, his majesty rode about as calmly as if he had been a British grenadier at Alma. Were I en-

I

gaged in fighting for my country, *I* should like such a suit of armor as
Prince Giglio wore ; but, you know, he was a prince of a fairy tale,
and they always have these wonderful things

Besides the fairy armor. the prince had a fairy horse, which would
gallop at any pace you please ; and a fairy sword, which would length-
en, and run through a whole regiment of enemies at once.   With such
a weapon at command, I wonder, for my part, he thought of order-
ing his army out, but forth they all came, in magnificent new uni-
forms ; Hedzoff and the prince's two college friends each command-
ing a division, and his majesty prancing in person at the head of
them all.

Ah ! if I had the pen of a Sir Archibald Alison, my dear friends,
would I not now entertain you with the account of a most tremendous shindy ?   Should not fine blows be struck ? dreadful wounds be
delivered ? arrows darken the air ? cannon balls crash through the
battalions ? cavalry charge infantry ? infantry pitch into cavalry ?
bugles blow ; drums beat ; horses neigh ; fifes ring ; soldiers roar,
swear, hurray ; officers shout out. " Forward, my men !" " This way,
lads !" "Give it 'em, boys. Fight for King Giglio, and the cause of
right !" " King Padella forever ?"   Would I not describe all this, I
say, and in the very finest language too ?   But this humble pen does
not possess the skill necessary for the description of combats.   In a
word, the overthrow of King Padella's army was so complete, that if
they had been Russians you could not have wished them to be more
utterly smashed and confounded.

As for that usurping monarch, having performed acts of valor much
more considerable than could be expected of a royal ruffian and usurper, who had such a bad cause, and who was so cruel to women—as
for King Padella, I say, when his army ran away, the king ran away
too. kicking his first general, Prince Punchikoff, from his saddle, and
galloping away on the prince's horse, having, indeed, had twenty-five
or twenty-six of his own shot under him.   Hedzoff coming up. and

THE TERRIFIC COMBAT BETWEEN KING GIGLIO AND PADELLA

finding Punchikoff down, as you may imagine very speedily disposed
of *him*.   Meanwhile King Padella was scampering off as hard as his
horse could lay legs to ground.   Fast as he scampered, I promise you
somebody else galloped faster; and that individual, as no doubt you
are aware, was the Royal Giglio, who kept bawling out, " Stay, trait-
or!   Turn, miscreant, and defend thyself!   Stand, tyrant, coward, ruffian, royal wretch, till I cut thy ugly head from thy usurping shoulders!"   And, with his fairy sword, which elongated itself at will, his
majesty kept poking and prodding Padella in the back, until that wicked monarch roared with anguish.

When he was fairly brought to bay, Padella turned and dealt Prince
Giglio a prodigious crack over the sconce with his battle-axe, a most
enormous weapon, which had cut down I don't know how many regi-
ments in the course of the afternoon.   But, law bless you! though
the blow fell right down on his majesty's helmet, it made no more
impression than if Padella had struck him with a pat of butter:
his battle-axe crumpled up in Padella's hand, and the royal Giglio
laughed for very scorn at the impotent efforts of that atrocious usurper.

At the ill success of his blow the Crim Tartar monarch was justly irritated.   " If," says he to Giglio, " you ride a fairy horse, and
wear fairy armor, what on earth is the use of my hitting you?   I
may as well give myself up a prisoner at once.   Your majesty won't,
I suppose, be so mean as to strike a poor fellow who can't strike
again?"

The justice of Padella's remark struck the magnanimous Giglio.
" Do you yield yourself a prisoner, Padella?" says he.

" Of course I do," says Padella.

" Do you acknowledge Rosalba as your rightful queen, and give up
the crown and all your treasures to your rightful mistress?"

" If I must I must," says Padella, who was naturally very sulky.

By this time King Giglio's aides-de-camp had come up, whom his
majesty ordered to bind the prisoner.   And they tied his hands be-

hind him, and bound his legs tight under his horse, having set him with his face to the tail; and in this fashion he was led back to King Giglio's quarters, and thrust into the very dungeon where young Bulbo had been confined.

Padella (who was a very different person, in the depth of his distress, to Padella, the proud wearer of the Crim Tartar crown) now most affectionately and earnestly asked to see his son—his dear eldest boy—his darling Bulbo; and that good-natured young man never once reproached his haughty parent for his unkind conduct the day before, when he would have left Bulbo to be shot without any pity, but came to see his father, and spoke to him through the grating of the door, beyond which he was not allowed to go; and brought him some sandwiches from the grand supper which his majesty was giving above stairs, in honor of the brilliant victory which had just been achieved.

"I can not stay with you long, sir," says Bulbo, who was in his best ball dress, as he handed his father in the prog; "I am engaged to dance the next quadrille with her majesty Queen Rosalba, and I hear the fiddles playing at this very moment."

So Bulbo went back to the ball-room, and the wretched Padella ate his solitary supper in silence and tears.

All was now joy in King Giglio's circle. Dancing, feasting, fun, illuminations, and jollifications of all sorts ensued. The people through whose villages they passed were ordered to illuminate their cottages at night, and scatter flowers on the roads during the day. They were requested, and I promise you they did not like to refuse, to serve the troops liberally with eatables and wine; besides, the army was enriched by the immense quantity of plunder which was found in King Padella's camp, and taken from his soldiers, who (after they had given up every thing) were allowed to fraternize with the conquerors, and the united armies marched back by easy stages toward King Giglio's capital, his royal banner and that of Queen Rosalba being carried in front of the troops. Hedzoff was made a duke and a field marshal. Smith and Jones were promoted to be earls; the Crim Tartar Order of the Pumpkin, and the Paflagonian decoration of the Cucumber, were freely distributed by their majesties to the army. Queen Rosalba wore the Paflagonian Ribbon of the Cucumber across her riding habit, while King Giglio never appeared without the grand Cordon of the Pumpkin. How the people cheered them as they rode along, side by side! They were pronounced to be the handsomest couple ever seen; that was a matter of course; but they really *were* very handsome, and, had they been otherwise, would have looked so, they were so happy! Their majesties were never separated during the whole day, but breakfasted, dined, and supped together always, and rode side by side, interchanging elegant compliments, and indulging in the most delightful conversation. At night, her majesty's ladies of honor (who had all rallied round her the day after King Padella's defeat) came and conducted her to the apartments prepared for her, while King Giglio, surrounded by his gentlemen, withdrew to his own royal quarters. It was agreed they should be married as soon as they reached the capital, and orders were dispatched to the Archbishop of Blombodinga to hold himself in readiness to perform the interesting ceremony. Duke Hedzoff carried the message, and gave instructions to have the royal castle splendidly refurnished and painted afresh. The duke seized Glumboso, the ex-prime minister, and made him refund that considerable sum of money which the old scoundrel had secreted out of the late king's treasure. He also clapped Valoroso into prison (who, by the way, had been dethroned for some considerable period past), and when the ex-monarch weakly remonstrated, Hedzoff said. "A soldier, sir, knows but his duty; my orders are to lock you up along with the ex-king Padella, whom I have brought hither a prisoner under guard." So these two ex-royal personages were sent for a year to the House of Correction, and thereafter were obliged to become monks of the severest Order of Flagel-

lants, in which state, by fasting, by vigils, by flogging (which they
administered to one another, humbly, but resolutely), no doubt they
exhibited a repentance for their past misdeeds, usurpations, and private and public crimes.

As for Glumboso, that rogue was sent to the galleys, and never had
an opportunity to steal any more.

XVIII.

HOW THEY ALL JOURNEYED BACK TO THE CAPITAL.

THE Fairy Blackstick, by whose means this young king and queen had certainly won their respective crowns back, would come, not unfrequently, to pay them a little visit—as they were riding in their triumphal process toward Giglio's capital—change her wand into a pony, and travel by their majesties' side, giving them the very best advice. I am not sure that King Giglio did not think the fairy and her advice rather a bore, fancying it was his own valor and merits which had put him on his throne, and conquered Padella; and, in fine, I fear he rather gave himself airs toward his best friend and patroness. She exhorted him to deal justly by his subjects, to draw mildly on the taxes, never to break his promise when he had once given it, and in all respects to be a good king.

"A good king, my dear fairy!" cries Rosalba. "Of course he will. Break his promise! Can you fancy my Giglio would ever do any thing so improper—so unlike him? No, never!" And she looked fondly toward Giglio, whom she thought a pattern of perfection.

"Why is Fairy Blackstick always advising me, and telling me how to manage my government, and warning me to keep my word? Does she suppose that I am not a man of sense and a man of honor?" asks Giglio, testily. "Methinks she rather presumes upon her position."

"Hush! dear Giglio," says Rosalba. "You know Blackstick has

been very kind to us, and we must not offend her." But the fairy
was not listening to Giglio's testy observations ; she had fallen back,
and was trotting on her pony now by Master Bulbo's side, who rode
a donkey, and made himself generally beloved in the army by his
cheerfulness, kindness, and good humor to every body. He was eager
to see his darling Angelica. He thought there never was such a
charming being. Blackstick did not tell him it was the possession
of the Magic Rose that made Angelica so lovely in his eyes. She
brought him the very best accounts of his little wife, whose misfortunes and humiliations had indeed very greatly improved her, and you
see she could whisk off on her wand a hundred miles in a minute,
and be back in no time, and so carry polite messages from Bulbo to
Angelica, and from Angelica to Bulbo, and comfort that young man
upon his journey.

When the royal party arrived at the last stage before you reach
Blombodinga, who should be in waiting, in her carriage there, with
her lady of honor by her side, but the Princess Angelica. She rushed
into her husband's arms, scarcely stopping to make a passing courtesy
to the king and queen. She had no eyes but for Bulbo, who appeared
perfectly lovely to her on account of the fairy ring which he wore ;
while she herself, wearing the magic rose in her bonnet, seemed entirely beautiful to the enraptured Bulbo.

A splendid luncheon was served to the royal party, of which the
archbishop, the chancellor, Duke Hedzoff, Countess Gruffanuff, and all
our friends partook, the Fairy Blackstick being seated on the left of
King Giglio, with Bulbo and Angelica beside her. You could hear the
joy-bells ringing in the capital, and the guns which the citizens were
firing off in honor of their majesties.

" What can have induced that hideous old Gruffanuff to dress herself up in such an absurd way ? Did you ask her to be your brides-
maid, my dear?" says Giglio to Rosalba. " What a figure of fun
Gruffy is !"

Gruffy was seated opposite their majesties, between the archbishop and the lord chancellor, and a figure of fun she certainly was, for she was dressed in a low white silk dress, with lace over, a wreath of white roses on her wig, a splendid lace veil, and her yellow old neck was covered with diamonds. She ogled the king in such a manner that his majesty burst out laughing.

"Eleven o'clock!" cries Giglio, as the great Cathedral bell of Blombodinga tolled that hour. "Gentlemen and ladies, we must be starting. Archbishop, you must be at church, I think, before twelve!"

"We must be at church before twelve," sighs out Gruffanuff, in a languishing voice, hiding her old face behind her fan.

"And then I shall be the happiest man in my dominions," cries Giglio, with an elegant bow to the blushing Rosalba.

"O my Giglio! O my dear majesty!" exclaims Gruffanuff; "and can it be that this happy moment at length has arrived—"

"Of course it has arrived," says the king.

"—And that I am about to become the enraptured bride of my adored Giglio!" continues Gruffanuff. "Lend me a smelling-bottle, somebody. I certainly shall faint with joy."

"You my bride!" roars out Giglio.

"You marry my prince!" cries poor little Rosalba.

"Pooh! Nonsense! The woman's mad!" exclaims the king. And all the courtiers exhibited by their countenances and expressions marks of surprise, or ridicule, or incredulity, or wonder.

"I should like to know who else is going to be married, if I am not?" shrieks out Gruffanuff. "I should like to know if King Giglio is a gentleman, and if there is such a thing as justice in Paflagonia! Lord chancellor! my lord archbishop! will your lordships sit by and see a poor, fond, confiding, tender creature put upon? Has not Prince Giglio promised to marry his Barbara? Is not this Giglio's signature? Does not this paper declare that he is mine, and only mine?" And she handed to his grace the archbishop the document which the prince

signed that evening when she wore the magic ring, and Giglio drank
so much champagne. And the old archbishop, taking out his eye-
glasses, read, " This is to give notice, that I, Giglio, only son of Savio,
King of Paflagonia, hereby promise to marry the charming Barbara
Griselda, Countess Gruffanuff, and widow of the late Jenkins Grufla-
nuff, Esq.' "

" H'm," says the archbishop, " the document is certainly a—a document."

" Phoo!" says the lord chancellor, " the signature is not in his majesty's hand-writing." Indeed, since his studies at Bosforo, Giglio had
made an immense improvement in caligraphy.

" Is it your hand-writing, Giglio ?" cries the Fairy Blackstick, with
an awful severity of countenance.

" Y—y—y—es," poor Giglio gasps out, " I had quite forgotten the
confounded paper : she can't mean to hold me by it. You old wretch,
what will you take to let me off? Help the queen, some one—her
majesty has fainted."

" Chop her head off !"   ) exclaim the impetuous Hedzoff, the
" Smother the old witch !"   } ardent Smith, and the faithful
" Pitch her into the river !"   ) Jones.

But Gruffanuff flung her arms round the archbishop's neck, and bel-
lowed out, " Justice, justice, my lord chancellor !" so loudly, that her
piercing shrieks caused every body to pause. As for Rosalba, she was
borne away lifeless by her ladies ; and you may imagine the look of
agony which Giglio cast toward that lovely being, as his hope, his joy,
his darling, his all in all, was thus removed, and in her place the horrid old Gruffanuff rushed up to his side, and once more shrieked out,
" Justice, justice !"

" Won't you take that sum of money which Glumboso hid ?" says
Giglio, " two hundred and eighteen thousand millions, or thereabouts.
It's a handsome sum."

" I will have that and you too !" says Gruffanuff.

"Let us throw the crown jewels into the bargain," gasps out Giglio.

"I will wear them by my Giglio's side!" says Gruffanuff.

"Will half, three quarters, five sixths, nineteen twentieths of my kingdom do, countess?" asks the trembling monarch.

"What were all Europe to me without *you*, my Giglio!" cries Gruff, kissing his hand.

"I won't, I can't, I s'an't; I'll resign the crown first," shouts Giglio, tearing away his hand; but Gruff clung to it.

"I have a competency, my love," she says, "and with thee and a cottage thy Barbara will be happy."

Giglio was half mad with rage by this time. "I will not marry her," says he. "Oh, fairy, fairy, give me counsel!" And as he spoke he looked wildly round at the severe face of the Fairy Blackstick.

"'Why is Fairy Blackstick always advising me, and warning me to keep my word? Does she suppose that I am not a man of honor?'" said the fairy, quoting Giglio's own haughty words. He quailed under the brightness of her eyes; he felt that there was no escape for him from that awful inquisition.

"Well, archbishop," said he, in a dreadful voice, that made his grace start, "since this fairy has led me to the height of happiness but to dash me down into the depths of despair, since I am to lose Rosalba, let me at least keep my honor. Get up, countess, and let us be married; I can keep my word, but I can die afterward."

"O dear Giglio," cries Gruffanuff, skipping up, "I knew—I knew I could trust thee—I knew that my prince was the soul of honor. Jump into your carriages, ladies and gentlemen, and let us go to church at once; and as for dying, dear Giglio, no, no—thou wilt forget that insignificant little chambermaid of a queen—thou wilt live to be consoled by thy Barbara! She wishes to be a queen, and not a queen dowager, my gracious lord!" and, hanging upon poor Giglio's arm, and leering and grinning in his face in the most disgusting manner, this old wretch tripped off in her white satin shoes, and jumped into the very carriage which had been got ready to convey Giglio and Rosalba to church. The cannons roared again, the bells pealed triple-bobmajors, the people came out, flinging flowers upon the path of the royal bride and bridegroom, and Gruff looked out of the gilt coach window and bowed and grinned to them. Phoo! the horrid old wretch!

XIX.

AND NOW WE COME TO THE LAST SCENE IN THE PANTOMIME.

THE many ups and downs of her life had given the Princess Rosalba prodigious strength of mind, and that highly principled young woman presently recovered from her fainting-fit, out of which Fairy Blackstick, by a precious essence which the fairy always carried in her pocket, awakened her. Instead of tearing her hair, crying and bemoaning herself, and fainting again, as many young women would have done, Rosalba remembered that she owed an example of firmness to her subjects, and though she loved Giglio more than her life, was determined, as she told the fairy, not to interfere between him and justice, or to cause him to break his royal word.

"I can not marry him, but I shall love him always," says she to Blackstick; "I will go and be present at his marriage with the countess, and sign the book, and wish them happy with all my heart. I will see, when I get home, whether I can not make the new queen some handsome presents. The Crim Tartary crown diamonds are uncommonly fine, and I never shall have any use for them. I will live and die unmarried, like Queen Elizabeth, and, of course, I shall leave my crown to Giglio when I quit this world. Let us go and see them married, my dear fairy; let me say one last farewell to him; and then, if you please, I will return to my own dominions."

So the fairy kissed Rosalba with peculiar tenderness, and at once changed her wand into a very comfortable coach and four, with a steady coachman, and two respectable footmen behind, and the fairy and Rosalba got into the coach, while Angelica and Bulbo entered after them. As for honest Bulbo, he was blubbering in the most pathetic manner, quite overcome by Rosalba's misfortune. She was touched by the honest fellow's sympathy, promised to restore to him the confiscated estates of Duke Padella his father, and created him, as he sat there in the coach, prince, highness, and first grandee of the Crim Tartar empire. The coach moved on, and, being a fairy coach, soon came up with the bridal procession.

Before the ceremony at church, it was the custom in Paflagonia, as it is in other countries, for the bride and bridegroom to sign the contract of marriage, which was to be witnessed by the chancellor, minister, lord mayor, and principal officers of state. Now, as the royal palace was being painted and furnished anew, it was not ready for the reception of the king and his bride, who proposed at first to take up their residence at the prince's palace—that one which Valoroso occupied when Angelica was born, and before he usurped the throne.

So the marriage party drove up to the palace; the dignitaries got out of their carriages and stood aside; poor Rosalba stepped out of her coach, supported by Bulbo, and stood almost fainting up against the railings, so as to have a last look of her dear Giglio. As for Blackstick, she, according to her custom, had flown out of the coach window in some inscrutable manner, and was now standing at the palace door.

Giglio came up the steps with his horrible bride on his arm, looking as pale as if he was going to execution. He only frowned at the Fairy Blackstick—he was angry with her, and thought she came to insult his misery.

"Get out of the way, pray," says Gruffanuff, haughtily. "I wonder why you are always poking your nose into other people's affairs!"

"Are you determined to make this poor young man unhappy?" says Blackstick.

MADAM GRUFFANUFF FINDS A HUSBAND.

"To marry him, yes! What business is it of yours? Pray, madam, don't say ' you' to a queen," cries Gruffanuff.

"You won't take the money he offered you?"

"No."

"You won't let him off his bargain, though you know you cheated him when you made him sign the paper?"

"Impudence! Policemen, remove this woman!" cries Gruffanuff. And the policemen were rushing forward, but with a wave of her wand the fairy struck them all like so many statues in their places.

"You won't take any thing in exchange for your bond, Mrs. Gruffanuff?" cries the fairy, with awful severity. "I speak for the last time."

"No!" shrieks Gruffanuff, stamping with her foot. "I'll have my husband—my husband—my husband!"

"You SHALL HAVE YOUR HUSBAND!" the Fairy Blackstick cried; and, advancing a step, laid her hand upon the nose of the KNOCKER.

As she touched it, the brass nose seemed to elongate, the open mouth opened still wider, and uttered a roar which made every body start. The eyes rolled wildly, the arms and legs uncurled themselves, writhed about, and seemed to lengthen with each twist; the knocker expanded into a figure in yellow livery, six feet high; the screws by which it was fixed to the door unloosed themselves, and JENKINS GRUFFANUFF once more trod the threshold off which he had been lifted more than twenty years ago!

"Master's not at home," says Jenkins, just in his old voice: and Mrs. Jenkins, giving a dreadful youp, fell down in a fit, in which nobody minded her.

For every body was shouting "Huzzay! huzzay!" "Hip, hip, hurray!" "Long live the king and queen!" "Were such things ever seen?" "No, never, never, never!" "The Fairy Blackstick forever!"

The bells were ringing double peals, the guns roaring and banging most prodigiously. Bulbo was embracing every body ; the lord chancellor was flinging up his wig and shouting like a madman ; Hedzoff had got the archbishop round the waist, and they were dancing a jig for joy ; and as for Giglio, I leave you to imagine what *he* was doing, and if he kissed Rosalba once, twice—twenty thousand times, I'm sure I don't think he was wrong.

So Gruffanuff opened the hall door with a low bow, just as he had been accustomed to do, and they all went in and signed the book, and then they went to church and were married, and the Fairy Blackstick sailed away on her cane, and was never more heard of in Paflagonia.

AND HERE ENDS THE FIRESIDE PANTOMIME.

www.ingramcontent.com/pod-product-compliance
Lightning Source LLC
Chambersburg PA
CBHW021136020726
47500CB00003B/1103